Filthy
Rich
Part 1

Kendall Banks

Life Changing Books in conjunction with Power Play Media

Published by Life Changing Books

P.O. Box 423 Brandywine, MD 20613

Library of Congress Cataloging-in-Publication Data;

www.lifechangingbooks.net

13 Digit: 978-1934230503
10 Digit: 1-934230502

Also By Kendall Banks

Filthy Rich (Part 2)
Rich Girls
One Night Stand
Another One Night Stand
Welfare Grind Part 1
Still Grindin' Part 2
Welfare Grind Part 3
Mistress Loose

Dedication

This book is dedicated to my readers. I owe a debt of gratitude to you for your love and continuous support. Thank you from the bottom of my heart.

Acknowledgements

Thank you to everyone who has inspired me, influenced me, or contributed to my success as an author in any way. Writing a book is a long journey and hard work…actually no matter how many books you write, it never gets easier. I consider myself extremely blessed to be a part of such an amazing team (LCB). A special thanks will forever go to Tressa "Azarel" Smallwood. Thanks for believing in me many years ago and thanks for enthusiastically supporting all of my new projects. There are not enough words to express my gratitude for everything you've done. To my entire family…you've given me more support than I could ever imagine and for that I love you for life!!!

XOXOXO,

Kendall Banks
Facebook: /authorkendallb
Twitter: @authorkendallb
Instagram: authorkendallb

Dear Diary

Tonight was on the money…The sex was great…The tongue even better. Still…my boo better step up. The stakes are getting higher. He promised to get all my needs fulfilled. It's just not coming fast enough.

Chapter 1

Her build was slim but curvaceous and athletically toned…her stomach washboard smooth. She was the woman most men craved. With long, jet-black, 26" weave draping below her shoulders she seemed perfect...like a sweet, petite goddess. Her light brown skin and thick lips made her assailants second guess their mission. After all, she was supposed to be family.

She was beautiful.

Her beauty couldn't be seen though at this particular moment. It was buried deeply underneath pain, bruises, scars, cuts, blood and tears. She looked nothing like the woman she had always prided herself on being.

Nessa's weave now had no body or shape. It was now heavily matted and dangled wildly over her entire blemished face. Her left eye was swollen and completely shut while her right eye contained semi-blurred vision. Her nose felt like it was broken, making it difficult for her to breathe as blood poured endlessly from both nostrils. Yet she never whined or complained. Her lips were swollen, dry and cracked while blood ran from the slit in her bottom lip. Her fingernails were missing; torturously ripped from her fingers with pliers by her captors. There was absolutely no beauty left to her.

Nessa's body was now as weak as that of a newborn baby. She had no fight left in her and couldn't stand on her own as the two gunmen dragged her stumbling through the dark woods. Overhead, beams of moonlight dimly illuminated the path in front of them. Her bare feet were becoming more and more soiled with dirt while her sweat soaked her body and clothes. Broken branches snapped underneath them while also piercing her soles so deeply they drew blood, too.

"All you had to do was talk, bitch," one of the goons told her.

He was dressed in a wife beater that exposed his muscular arms covered from wrist to shoulder in gruesome looking scars. Wearing a pair of crispy blue Dickies that sagged his Polo boxers were exposed. On his feet were a pair of white Shell-toed Adidas. In his free hand was a chrome Glock that he intended on using to destroy Nessa for good.

"Yeah, bitch," the gunman on Nessa's left side belted, agreeing with his partner. He was just as muscular as the other man but more thuggish. In his free hand was a black .45 that he'd suddenly decided to press against Nessa's head.

"Got to hand it to you though," he continued. "You're a strong one; real strong. Most bitches fold after only a minute. You got balls, bitch. "

"Hell yeah," the other agreed.

"You though, you hung in there. You went out like a soldier."

Their voices were dripping with sarcasm, not admiration.

Nessa was nearly drifting in and out of consciousness as the men spoke to her. The pain nearly killed her. It was torture. Making her actually wish and yearn for death as she drifted into unconsciousness again. Her mind played back everything from the moment her captors caught her.

The two men had caught Nessa coming out of the hair salon. As she hit the unlock button on the key to her tinted out black Range Rover, a white cargo van emerged out of nowhere and skidded to a stop behind her. Before she could react its side door slid open and two masked men jumped out. In the blink of an eye they had her in their arms with a hand over her mouth and tossed her inside. The next several hours were the most brutal and terrifying she'd ever experienced or endured.

"Where the fuck Luke's stash houses at?" was one of the questions Nessa was asked over and over again.

"Fuck you!" she returned countless times, even spitting in one of the captors' face once when he got too close.

Nessa wasn't weak. She wasn't soft. She had a past full of violence and had crazy survival skills. She'd been born and bred to be loyal. The term "Death Before Dishonor" meant something special to her. She even had it tattooed in old English letters across her bikini line. For her, those words weren't just a phrase. They were a way of life, especially when it came to the most important man in her life...

Luke.

Luke and his family were the most successful crime family Washington D.C. had ever seen. They were a family of multimillionaires who ran each of their enterprises with an iron fist. Disrespect wasn't tolerated. Fear among their soldiers wasn't accepted. Talking to the police was a mandatory death sentence.

They weren't a joke.

Nessa was Luke's heart. She was both his queen and princess. He kept a plush roof over her head and her pock-

4

ets loaded. *The rare diamonds around her wrists and neck couldn't be rivaled by many. Luke had real money...old and new. He kept the most expensive clothes and fabrics on Nessa's skin and the newest designer heels and sandals on her pedicured feet.*

He loved her but beyond measure.

It was because of that love that Nessa would never tell on him or his family. She didn't care who was asking. It didn't matter if those infiltrators were killers or the Feds themselves. She'd die before turning over on Luke. And during the current moment, it looked like dying was exactly what she was going to do.

For hours in the dirty basement that smelled of mildew and piss, the torture and abuse continued. As a light bulb dangled by a thin wire from overhead, she was beaten, choked, slapped, kicked and spat on. All of it occurred as she sat helpless in a wooden chair with her wrists and ankles duct taped to it.

"Talk, bitch!" one of the men yelled just before punching her in the face so hard she thought her jaw was broken. "Where the fuck his stash houses at?"

Dazed and barely able to lift her chin from her breasts, she said weakly, "Eat a dick, bitch!"

Looking at his partner, the goon laughed and said, "Whoaaaaaaaaaaa, she's got balls. Eat a dick, huh?"

With her chin in her chest and looking up at him through her matted hair and swollen eye, she said, "What, you deaf, muthafucka? Yeah, I said eat a dick."

The two men laughed again. One of them then unzipped his pants, freed his dick and said, "Naw, bitch. How 'bout you drink some piss?" He then began to urinate all over her. By the time he was finished, piss had drenched her weave and tank top. Its stench smelled so bad she threw up all over the floor.

5

Filthy Rich BY: KENDALL BANKS

"We can do this all night, bitch," he told her as he placed his dick back in his pants and zipped up. "I don't have any place to be. And you just might get raped in this muthafucka if you don't talk soon."

Several moments passed by. Nessa feared getting raped but still remained silent. Soon, more punches battered Nessa's face.

"Talk, hoe!" the gunman demanded as he struck Nessa in the stomach.

Coughing and gasping for air, Nessa said, "Okay, okay, I'll…I'll…"

"You'll what?" he asked, pressing his ear close to her face.

"I'll talk," she told him. "I…I promise, I'll talk."

Looking at his partner with a grin, he said, "Alright, bitch, talk. Tell us what we want to hear. Tell us where the fuck Luke keeps all that bread."

With pain and torment evident in her voice, she told him, "The…the…the next time…I'm…"

Both men listened carefully.

"The next time…I'm…I'm on my period, eat my bloody pussy, bitch ass nigga. How's that? Is that what your soft ass wanted to hear?" She then laughed wildly. Her ribs ached terribly. But she forced the laughter.

Growing infuriated, the goon punched her twice. "You think this is a game, bitch? You think we're playing?" He pulled his gun out and prepared to pistol whip her until his partner stopped him.

Instead…More punches.

After several minutes, he said, "Alright, I've got something for you." He then pulled a pair of pliers from his back pocket.

Nessa weakly raised her throbbing head to see them.

6

"Let's see if this gets you to talk."

The man then latched the mouth of the pliers to the nail of Nessa's forefinger and began to pull until it ripped from its roots.

Nessa screamed at the top of her lungs in pain. Tears flowed from her eyes as she breathed heavily.

"Talk, bitch!"

She formed an even more stern face yet stayed silent as the tears continued to flow.

Another nail was ripped from her hand. She screamed even louder than before. The pain was unbearable. She'd never felt anything so excruciating.

"Where the fucking money at? Just tell us about one stash house and we'll let you live."

"Fuck you, muthafucka. Kill me!" she shouted.

Another slap.

Another punch.

"Kill me," she screamed. "Kill me, muthafuckas. And after you do, kill yourselves. Because when Luke finds out what you've done there won't be a place on earth your scum ass will be able to hide!"

With an open hand she was smacked viciously and knocked to the ground.

The slap brought Nessa back to current reality...still in the dark, creepy woods. The men now had her between them as they stood at what looked like a freshly dug grave. She was too weak to raise her head and didn't want to open her useable eye.

"Pay attention, bitch," the gunman who'd slapped her ordered. "This is the good part. You don't want to miss your own damn funeral, do you?"

From over the pit, Nessa looked down into it to see an opened casket sitting at the bottom. Inside the casket was a body covered in blood. Its eyes were open and staring directly up at her. Nessa immediately panicked.

Feeling and sensing her fear, both men laughed.

"Don't worry 'bout him, baby girl," one of them said. "We just put his ass in there to keep you company. He ain't gon' bite. He dead already."

They laughed again.

"Alright, bitch, last chance," she was told. "You want to tell us where those stash houses are? That's all it takes. Tell us what we want; we let you go 'bout your business."

Silently, Nessa saw Luke's face in her head. She heard his voice. All his motivational words…his loving words. She felt his kisses. She remembered the first time they met. She remembered their love making. She knew exactly where he kept most of his money and where his major stash houses were located. She could easily reveal the details and live. But each thought and memory made her tell her captors one final time…

"Fuck you."

She refused to turn on her man.

Shaking their heads, both men said almost at the exact same time, "Suit yourself then. You's a dead bitch, now."

With those words said, she was shoved into the pit and into the casket. Her body crashed down on the chest of the dead man as she screamed loudly.

"Noooooooooooo! Fuck Nooooooo! Don't do thisssssssss!"

She and he were now eye to eye. Her insides shook and bile rose up in her gut.

The casket shut.

Nessa vomited once again.

Darkness dominated.

Nessa, although hardened by the many things she'd

8

experienced in life, broke down. She'd been taught to survive through several foster homes, abduction, family deaths, and violence at the hand of an old love, but nothing to this extreme. She couldn't help sobbing as she heard the dirt crashing down on the roof of the casket. Knowing she was going to be buried alive had her body shaking and her heart pounding.

As moment after moment passed by, she thought about Luke. She was dying inside knowing she'd never see him again. She wished she could tell him she loved him one last time. She wished she could kiss him one more time. She wished he had come to his senses and agreed to marry her before now.

More dirt crashed down.

Seconds seemed like hours.

Besides the vomit, the blood of the dead man underneath her turned her stomach. She could smell it. In fact, it wasn't a *smell*. It was a stench. It sickened her terribly. She wanted to cover her nostrils but her arms were far too weak. She could only lay there.

And wait to die.

A slow death.

Moments passed.

More dirt crashing down sounded.

More moments passed.

Suddenly…

Silence.

Nessa wondered why the sound of falling dirt had ceased. She listened closely. She could hear voices but couldn't make out what they were saying.

Then more silence.

Then…

The casket opened.

A shot gun was now in sight.

Moonlight immediately flooded the pit. Nessa, still in the most pain she'd ever experienced in her life, mustered up the strength to raise her head from the dead man's chest. Slightly, she turned to look toward the top of the pit. What she saw staring down at her both frightened and confused her...

Those eyes.

Those green eyes.

Was it really him?

Filthy Rich BY: KENDALL BANKS

Chapter 2

The tinted black S550 Mercedes Benz gracefully slithered through D.C. a little after one a.m. Underneath the night's full moon and glistening stars, the luxury whip passed by war-torn, battered-beyond-repair neighborhoods. Vacant buildings, lots and store fronts lined main streets. Abandoned houses, unkempt lawns, and busted out streetlamps lined side streets. The neighborhoods were a far cry from the city's bustling and brightly lit downtown. The west side seemed like the land that time forgot.

Despite the time of night, the neighborhood's worst of the worst and most disappointing roamed its streets and sidewalks. Crackheads and prostitutes walked the shadows on missions to find money to feed their drug habits. Their faces and bodies showed the ravaging consequences of years of addiction and abuse. Dope boys, most young and strapped with guns, stood on corners anxious to sell them the poison they chased endlessly day and night. From distances not too far away gunshots echoed along with blaring police sirens.

From the back seat of the Benz and from behind the darkness of the windows' tint, Luke stared out at the ghetto's hopeless and violent landscape in thought, knowing he was a huge reason why the entire city's black community had fallen into such turmoil. It was mainly the Heroin from his family's multimillion dollar Cocaine and Meth drug ring that flowed through their veins. It was his family's crack and marijuana that flooded their lungs. It was his family's guns that countless gangsters, including children, clutched while playing their part in running up the city's overwhelming murder rate.

Luke's family was undoubtedly the most successful family of kingpins Washington D.C. had seen since Rayful Edmonds. They hadn't achieved their success through only violence, intimidation and murder though. They'd also achieved it by building relationships and alliances with folks in high places. They had a man in the DEA. They had police officers on the take. They had a judge in their pocket. They were even due a few favors from the city's mayor because they had been a huge reason why the mayor won the election in the first place. During Mayor Walberg's campaign and electoral race, their family threatened and bullied voters into voting for him. The family also contributed thousands of dollars to the mayor's campaign. The assistance and influence resulted in a landslide win.

As Luke stared out of the car's window at the world around him, he felt more like a prisoner of his family's success than anything else. He felt more like a failure than an accomplished business man.

He felt like a criminal.

Somehow he hated the wealthy life and the past that led him to his current position. His family held so many secrets that most would puke, cry, and run for the hills if they got wind of what was taking place. Luke dropped his head and looked down at Nessa's battered and bruised face as it lay in his lap. Her eyes were closed. He grimaced at the sight as he began to rub her head softly. His eyes slowly roamed from her face down the entire length of her body. He saw bruises, cuts and blood. His nostrils smelled the stench of the blood and urine. He was sickened but not by what he saw. No; what sickened him was the part he him-self had played in her assault.

Luke had given the order.

It nearly destroyed Luke when he ordered his goons to test the loyalty of the woman he loved. Nessa was his lady, his ride or die, his bitch; his number one. It shattered his heart in countless pieces to have to give such an order. But just like so many other things he despised during his life in this business, it had to be done. He had no choice but to accept it and hope she would still love him after-ward. He had to be sure Nessa wasn't the insider feeding information to those after him.

Against his brother's fears, Luke had begun sharing private information about the family business over the last few months. He'd told her where he kept large sums of cash. She knew about a few of the stash houses. She knew workers, lawyers, contacts, and most of all, family secrets. Looking down at Nessa, Luke realized he'd made a good decision by trusting her.

The Mercedes turned off of a main street and into a dark alley. As the car's tires made their way down the alley's trash cluttered pavement, its headlight's brought into view a parked Cadillac Escalade. Two men were sit-ting inside; one in the driver's seat, the other in the passen-ger seat. Both goons had been the two who had inflicted Nessa's torture on her. After they dumped her in the makeshift grave, Luke sent them to handle crew business and then meet him here.

The brakes of the Benz's factory rimmed wheels squealed lightly as the car came to an abrupt stop. After

placing the whip in park, the driver stepped out and began
to make his way along the passenger side towards the trunk
and around to Luke's door. When he reached the door, he
opened it graciously.

Luke eased his thigh from underneath Nessa's head
and replaced it with the palm of his hand as he slid out of
the backseat. With his hand he lovingly rested her head
down on the seat. He then took off his suit jacket revealing
a shoulder holster and gun. His once white dress shirt was
now stained in Nessa's blood. The thighs of his pants were
also. He softly placed the suit coat over her. A moment
later he slipped his hands into a pair of plastic gloves.

Nessa, still dazed from her beating, mumbled something incoherently to Luke. "Shhhhhhh," he said, placing
his lips to her ear softly. "I'll be back shortly. I promise."
He then kissed her on the cheek affectionately and shut the
door.

Stuffing his hands into the pockets of his pants,
Luke and his driver headed towards the Escalade. Behind
them, The Mercedes's headlights shined illuminating the
area between them and the SUV. As they walked, the heels
of Luke's fourteen hundred dollar, Tom Ford loafers
clicked and echoed off the walls of the abandoned buildings lining both sides of the narrow alleyway. The two men
awaiting them in the SUV climbed out. Both groups of
men met up in front of the Escalade's hood.

"The two of you did an exceptional job tonight,"
Luke commended them while still keeping his hands in his
pockets. "You do good work."

Both goons looked at each other and smiled
proudly, glad that their work was to their bossman's liking.
Everyone wanted to please Luke at all times, no matter the
cost.

"I appreciate that," Luke told them.

"It was nothin'," one of the men replied. "Whatever you need done, you know we're always game for that shit."

"Really?" Luke asked, glaring at the huge gap between his teeth.

"That's right, boss."

"Even if I ordered you to smoke our boy here?"

The man turned to his partner with a sinister stare. Then looked back at Luke.

The moment became far too weird.

"It's all business, right?" he asked Luke then shrugged his shoulders.

Luke nodded. He then looked at his driver and said, "Pay these soldiers. They've done what I asked."

The driver reached into his suit jacket's inner pocket, pulled out an envelope and handed it to one of the goons. The goon didn't even bother to open it. With a smile on his face, he simply stuffed it in the front pocket of his jeans.

"You're not going to count it?" Luke asked.

"Nahhhh, you're good. We trust you."

"Important rule, gentlemen; never trust anyone."

The goons nodded.

With that said, Luke turned to head back to the Benz. His driver did also. After taking several steps, Luke stopped, turned and said as if he'd forgotten something, "Oh, gentlemen, one other thing?"

The two goons were heading around the hood of the Escalade as he spoke. They stopped and turned to him. "What's up, boss?"

Luke pulled his hands from his pockets, grabbed the gun from his holster, took aim at the man on the truck's driver side and squeezed the trigger.

Amidst the gun's thundering blast, its bullet tore

through the man's forehead and ripped the entire back of his skull off. Brain, skull and patches of hair scattered on the ground and the Escalade's driver's side door. The man crumpled to the ground.

"What the fuck?" the man on the passenger side said in surprise and disbelief. Fear quickly captured his entire face as his eyes went from where his partner was once standing to Luke.

Luke immediately took aim at him. With one last glare into the gap between his teeth he sighed. "Respect is everything."

Raising his hands in defense, his eyes wide, the goon asked, "What did I do?"

Without giving him an answer, Luke squeezed the trigger again. The back of the man's head exploded just like his partner's had done. He hit the ground a second later. Luke then walked over to the first man and stood over him. Blood spilled from the back of his skull and flowed endlessly. Luke, unfazed by the blood, let off three shots in the man's chest to insure he was dead. As he did, each shot was accompanied by bright flashes from the gun. Empty shell casings spilled from the side of the barrel onto the ground. Immediately after the last shot was fired, he headed around the hood to the second man. Seeing him lying on his back with half his head gone and his legs twitching, Luke fired three shots into his chest. The man's body went totally still.

Silence.

Brief moments passed.

Luke turned and walked back to his driver. The driver didn't say anything. He'd seen countless men murdered in this business, the game his employer was in. This one wasn't expected though. There had been no forewarning. Instead of saying a word though, he only looked at

Luke with a sort of bewildered stare. Knowing what the driver wanted to ask, Luke said to him, "No man should know how it feels to harm another man's woman and live."

With those words said, Luke handed the handle of the gun to the driver and said, "Get rid of the gun and the bodies. I'll drive myself home."

Taking off the rubber gloves, Luke headed to the Benz.

Filthy Rich BY: KENDALL BANKS

Chapter 3

The white stucco, three million dollar, two-storied mansion sat on 6.5 acres of breathtaking land in Potomac Maryland. It was surrounded by plush green lawns, a long circular drive way, a three-bedroom guest house, golf course, basketball court, and an Olympic sized swimming pool. Inside, it was laced with marble floors, towering high ceilings, eight bedrooms, six bathrooms, a movie theater, a butler, maid and so much more.

The Mercedes made its way up the cobble stone drive way and parked beneath the home's wide staircase. Luke shut off the car's engine and hopped out. Moments later, with Nessa in his arms, he made his way up the stairs toward the front door. Her head rested against his chest and her arms were wrapped around his shoulders as he walked. As he reached the top of the stairs, the home's fourteen foot French styled double doors opened. A man resembling Luke, only younger and with freshly done dreads appeared. He was dressed in a pair of Louis Vuitton high top sneakers, black Louis Vuitton jeans which sagged, and a white wife beater that revealed chiseled and exotically detailed tattoos from neck to shoulder. His name was Darien, Luke's little brother.

Stepping into the foyer, Luke asked his brother, "Are the doctor and nurse here yet?"

Darien looked at Nessa's battered body. "Yeah, they're in the main room."

"Good. Tell them to meet me upstairs in the master bedroom in ten minutes. I need a minute with her to myself."

Darien closed the door. "How'd she fend? I mean, is she ride or die, or nah?"

"She's everything I thought she was," Luke answered as he headed towards the sweeping staircase which was actually two separate staircases that curved towards each other as they rose and met at the top. In between them were a gorgeous fountain and a walkway that led to one of the house's two dens.

As Luke carried Nessa up the stairs, he noticed a striking woman standing at the second floor railing directly in the center of where the staircases met. Just like Darien, she bore resemblance to Luke, just older and feminine. Her name was Mrs. Bishop, Luke's mother, whom most called Chetti.

Chetti was a slim, Brazilian looking woman in her mid-fifties who carried herself more like a fiery woman in her thirties. Her long, naturally wavy hair, which hung to her elbows, had been dyed a bronze shade with bright blonde highlights, giving her the appearance of an islander. Her facial features, although obviously aged, still had an exotic look to them. Her brown eyes had a natural slant to them although there was no Asian blood anywhere in her family.

Holding a glass of expensive, imported Tequila, which she always drank straight; no chaser, Chetti was dressed in a black, lace embroidered La Perla night gown. Her pedicured feet were bare. The hair on the left side of her face purposely draped over her left eye and the entire left side of her face concealing it totally as she stared out over the first floor like a queen proudly surveying her empire.

Luke was nearly at the top of the stairs when his mother asked without looking at him, keeping her gaze over the railing, "What happened to her?" Her tone was cold, purposely designed to show she had no genuine concern for Nessa's current state. She'd never liked Nessa and wasn't going to start now.

Hearing the coldness in his mother's voice, Luke didn't answer her as he reached the top step.

Shrugging her shoulders and still gazing over the railing, she said, "Bitch probably deserved it. There's a reason why trash is best left in the streets." Her voice was filled with arrogance and privilege.

"Mother, don't speak on things you know nothing about," Luke told her as he passed behind her back.

Chetti's nostrils caught a strong whiff of the urine and blood radiating from Nessa's body when Luke walked by. Making a distasteful face, she said, "Even *smells* like trash." She took a sip of her Tequila and shook her head. Ice cubes clinked against the sides of the glass.

"Bitch," Nessa whispered with her face still resting against Luke's chest. Nessa hated Chetti just as much Chetti hated her.

Luke continued to ignore his mother as he made his way down the hall. Oddly, his mother had no idea how much Luke really disliked her. He respected and loved her, but detested her at the same time. When he reached the master bedroom and opened the door, from behind him she yelled, "I'll be sure to have the maid burn the sheets. Then I'll be sure to have her burn the fucking bed!"

Luke shut the door as his mother's arrogant laughter

began to fill the hall. He carried Nessa across the marble floor of the huge bedroom and laid her softly on the silk sheets of the king-sized bed they shared most nights. Sitting beside her, he gazed at her beauty silently.

Moments passed before Luke finally spoke. "You know this had to be done, right?"

Nessa might've been badly battered and bruised, but her ability to comprehend was fully in tact. She knew exactly what he meant.

Nessa's eye, the one that wasn't swollen shut, opened and looked up at Luke as he began to get up from the bed. She grabbed his arm. "Why?" she whispered with the back of her head resting on the lavish pillow. A tear began to roll down the side of her face.

Suddenly, there was a knock at the door.

"Give me a moment!" he shouted to the door, knowing it was the doctor and nurse who'd been waiting on standby to treat Nessa. He looked back down at her.

"Why?" she asked again, her voice still just above a whisper. She felt betrayed and her saddened face showed it. "Why did you do this to me? I thought you loved me."

Looking her directly in the eyes, Luke told her in a tone just a low as her own, "I did it *because* I love you."

Nessa didn't understand. Not at all. In the past she'd always trusted anything Luke told her. He was seventeen years older than Nessa and a lot wiser. Whatever plans he had for them, Nessa normally went along with it.

"If I didn't love you, you would be dead," he said. "I had to be sure I could trust you."

Nessa peered into the pair of mesmerizing green eyes she loved so much.

"Haven't I proved that already? Isn't my word enough?"

"*Now* it is. But you know people were finding out

things about me that no one should know."

"And so you thought it was me?" she asked hurt-fully.

The two fell silent.

A knock came from the door again.

"Come back in fifteen minutes!" Luke shouted.

Luke began to stroke the side of Nessa's face softly. "You're the most beautiful woman in this world to me," he said, truly meaning it. "Even your scars are beautiful."

"You mean that?"

The moment Luke grabbed a hold of Nessa's hands, guilt filled him again after seeing her finger's damaged nail beds. As usual, he felt like he needed to spoil Nessa. And in this case pay for torturing her.

Reaching into his pocket and pulling out several stacks, he said, "Here, take this for now. After the doctors fix you up nicely, I'm taking you to Paris. You're going to get everything you deserve and more."

Instantly, Nessa threw the stack of money to the side as if she didn't want it. She couldn't speak.

A tear fell.

Then another.

"You know what I want, Luke."

His eyes met hers as if there was some secret code between them.

Placing his face between her hands still covered in dried up blood, Luke heard Nessa say, "I need a shower then I want you to make love to me."

Luke kissed her softly. "No shower needed. I want you just the way you are."

He took off his empty shoulder holster, unbuttoned his blood stained shirt and threw it on the floor revealing a muscular chest and a six-pack laced stomach. He had no tattoos or scars. For a forty year old man, Luke was cut, especially in his upper body area.

Staring up into Luke's eyes, Nessa laid there as he undressed her delicately like an expensive doll. Knowing her body was fragile from the torture she'd suffered, he didn't want to hurt her. His compassion and thoughtfulness made her pussy wet. She wanted him inside her.

Luke, after getting Nessa undressed, began to kiss her lips. The taste of her blood didn't bother him at all. The stench of urine didn't turn his stomach. Whatever her pain or discomfort, he wanted to be a part of it. He wanted to join with her.

"I love you," she whispered into his ear as he began to plant gentle kisses around her neck.

"I love you, too," he whispered back.

"So, are you ready to marry me now?"

Luke's dick throbbed inside of his pants as he placed kisses all over her breasts. He didn't want to discuss marriage. He wanted to make love. He'd never wanted Nessa more than he wanted her right now. The feeling was intensifying.

"You hear me, Luke? I asked, are you ready to marry me now?"

Luke continued his foreplay session for several seconds before final telling Nessa, "Can we talk about this later? I want you, now."

Although her missing fingernails had her hands aching, Nessa bore the pain as she reached for the button of Luke's pants. She too had gotten extremely horny and wanted Luke inside of her. Quickly, Luke had taken off his clothes and watched as Nessa took hold of his dick, and began to stroke it.

"Ahhhhhhhh, baby," he moaned.

"You're everything in this world to me, Luke," she whispered into his ear.

"You too, baby girl," he returned.

Luke began to plant wet kisses on Nessa's stomach. As he did, he noticed the bruises on her belly, ribs and arms. He was face to face with them. Realizing Nessa had gone through the ultimate sacrifice for him and succeeded, he began licking her thighs and kissing her bruises. Nessa's right thigh was special to Luke. It was the leg that showcased the tattoo of his name, along with Nessa's choice of flowers and tiger paws.

"I love you so much, baby," Nessa whispered as she closed her eyes and basked in her man's kisses.

Luke worked his way down to Nessa's pussy, a place he visited often. He sucked her clit softly and gently causing it to swell and harden. He then placed her thighs over his shoulders, slipped his tongue inside the pussy and began to work it deeply.

"Oh Luke," she whispered as she grabbed onto his bald head.

Luke worked the pussy with his tongue even more vigorously. The taste was driving him crazy. He needed all of it. He had to *have* all of it. Getting a tighter grip on Nessa's thighs, he buried his face in her box as far as he could and began to lap out her tunnel so savagely his mouth made loud slurping sounds.

"Babyyyyy," she moaned as she arched her back up from the bed. Her toes curled. Her hands and fingers got a tighter grip on his skull. Her body still ached from the torture she'd endured earlier but the pleasure Luke was giving her seemed to drown it out.

Luke continued feasting.

Moments passed.

Suddenly…

A loud knock at the door.

"I'll tell you when I'm ready for you!" Luke yelled

26

back, figuring it was the doctor and nurse again.

Darien's voice came from behind the door. "It's me, nigga. It's important!"

Luke reluctantly climbed off of Nessa, threw on his pants and walked across the room to the door. Opening it, but using himself to block Nessa's naked body, he could tell by the look on his brother's face and the growing rage in his eyes something was wrong. "What is it?" he asked.

"It's bad," Darien told him with a silver chromed glock in his hand. He'd pulled his dreads into a tight pony-tail. "It's *real* fuckin' bad. We gotta go right now."

"Alright." Luke shut the door, grabbed his shirt and kissed Nessa. "I'll be back as soon as I can," he told her.

"Nooooo, Luke. Not now."

"Nessa, look, some people have been after me for a while. This is serious. Stay here. You'll be safe." Seconds later, he was gone.

Nessa lay on her back in a daze. Without Luke there to pleasure her, the pain of the beating and torture she took came back. It began to make her wince.

"Damn humanitarian project," Chetti said, leaning against the frame of the door looking at Nessa. She was still holding her glass of Tequila.

"What?" Nessa asked, pulling the sheets over her naked body.

"You're a humanitarian project for my son, a mercy fuck even. Just something to stick his dick in until the next one comes along."

"You know what, Chetti maybe that's what *your* damn problem is. Maybe you need some good dick shoved in that decrepit cobweb infested pussy of yours. Maybe if you got a mercy fuck or whatever kind of fuck, you'd be less of a bitch."

Chetti chuckled.

The two women went back and forth like this often, mainly behind Luke's back.

"You know what else I think your problem is?" Nessa asked.

"No, ghetto trash, enlighten me. Or better yet, crackbaby, *humor* me."

"You know that I'm more than just the latest bitch in Luke's long line of conquests. You see it in his eyes every time he looks at me. You hear it in his voice every time he talks *to* me or *about* me."

Chetti smirked.

"And you especially hear it in his moans when you're listening outside the door, which I know you do often with your sneaky ass. You hear him all up inside my pussy, don't you?"

Chetti's eyes narrowed.

Knowing she had gotten to Chetti, Nessa went further. She smiled and said, "It eats your miserable ass up inside to know that I'm next in line for *your* job. I'm next in line to be the queen of this family. And know that I'll be spending the millions that your husband left to you and your sons. As soon as they throw the dirt on your boney, decrepit, and dried up lookin' ass, I'll be calling the shots around here. Shit, I'm only twenty-three, I've got time to watch you die."

Unable to keep her composure, Chetti slammed her glass to the floor so hard it shattered. "Let me tell you something, you weave having video vixen reject," she said with fury in her eyes and face. "I've been running this family alongside my husband ever since your parents were standing in line during the Reagan era for government cheese. I've brokered more business deals than you can count. I've sent more motherfuckers to the poorhouse than the IRS. I've lunched with countless fashion designers in

28

Paris while the closest *you've* ever gotten to them is wearing that cheap-ass True Religion."

Nessa eyed her closely. She'd never seen her so furious.

"But most importantly, bitch, and pay attention because this is the part that really pertains directly to you," Chetti told her with a cold glare. "I've had more motherfuckers killed than The Vietnam War. I'm as lethal as poison. The fucking AIDS virus ain't got shit on me."

Nessa didn't speak. She knew the grimace on Luke's mother's face meant something wicked. Luke had shared with her some vicious things his mother had done to her enemies in the past. She wasn't to be fucked with.

"So if you've got eyes on my spot, hoe," Chetti continued, "I suggest you pick out a cemetery plot because I will personally be there to witness one of my goons put a bullet through the center of your head before I allow that. It's only because of the love I have for my son that you're alive this long or even living in this house. Don't get it twisted. I may be older than you but pushing your luck can be fatal when dealing with a bitch like me."

Suddenly, the doctor and nurse walked into the bedroom unannounced. Looking at them and smiling, Chetti said, "Get her fixed up very nicely. There's a tip in it for you. I want her to look just as good as new when she takes her one way trip back to the ghetto." She looked at Nessa and winked. A moment later, she was gone.

As the doctor and nurse began to tend to Nessa's wounds, the look on her face was a cold one as she kept her eyes locked on the spot where her new enemy had been standing. The old bitch had pissed her off countless times. They'd teed off more times than either of them could count. The little disagreements had never gotten to Nessa. This time though, it was different. It *had* gotten to her.

Nessa was far beyond pissed off. Chetti had threatened her life with intentions of scaring her off. Little did she know though her threat had birthed something relentless inside Nessa. Now as Nessa lay there in bed, she promised herself she was going to be the queen of the Bishop family no matter what it took.

Filthy Rich BY: KENDALL BANKS

Chapter 4

The engine of the yellow Aston Martin Vanquish with black trim growled menacingly as its tires sharply turned to the right causing it to whip up into the dark parking lot. As it headed toward the old abandoned bread factory in Northwest D.C., its headlights brought several parked SUVs into view, each of them parked side by side. Several men holding guns stood among them.

Gravel spurted from underneath the Aston Martin's tires as it headed directly toward the line of SUV's. Seconds later, it screeched to a halt. Quickly both its doors swung open. Darien hopped out of the driver's side while Luke emerged from the passenger side.

Approaching them, one of the awaiting gunmen said to them as they met up in front of the Aston Martin, "It's real fucked up in there." He shook his head as he spoke. "Some real live horror movie type shit."

Anger was all over Darien's face. His eyes were bloodshot with something far beyond rage. Darien definitely wasn't the type who took situations like this well and with a grain of salt. Luke on the other hand, was calm. The expression on his face showed no hint whatsoever of what he felt or thought. He never showed emotion, no matter the situation. Luke's motto was "Wise men think when super composed".

Pissed off, ignoring his soldier, Darien brushed passed him bumping his shoulder with such force he knocked him out of the way. He immediately headed for the factory with his eyes locked on its entrance. Nothing around him was worth even a morsel of interest at that moment. Luke and the rest of the soldiers followed behind him.

The factory was empty. The rows of wall to wall equipment that once filled the room had been removed shortly after it was shut down. It now smelled of mildew, urine, feces, and Lord knows whatever as the men entered inside. Decades worth of garbage littered the floors. Grime and mud soiled them also as syringes, discarded condoms, beer cans, shattered wine bottles and much more were scattered about. The walls were covered in graffiti.

"Where they at?" Darien asked as he now stood inside the factory with a heavy scowl on his face.

"Upstairs," a gunman told him.

Everyone headed up a set of iron stairs to the second floor. The soles of their shoes and boots echoed against the walls. As soon as they reached the top, death bombarded their nostrils. Dairen and Luke could actually smell the stench of blood. There was no mistaking it. They'd killed enough men to know exactly how it smelled. Right now its stench was thick and heavy. Its nauseating smell though was nothing compared to the sight awaiting them.

Darien froze.

Luke stood beside his brother.

Their eyes stared at the mayhem and bloodshed in front of them.

As moonlight shined into the second floor through

the frames' broken windows, several men were scattered about the floor dead. They weren't just dead though; they were posed in humiliating and degrading positions. One of them was bent at the waist over a table with his arms outstretched. Nails had been driven into the backs of his hands through his palms to pin him to the table. His jeans and boxers were pulled down around his ankles. A broken broom stick had been shoved into his rectum; the broken end first.

Another man hung from the rafters by his neck. A rope was tied around his neck. His body was completely naked. His hands were tied behind his back. His eyes, although lifeless, were wide open as they stared off into the distance ahead of him while his head leaned limply across his left shoulder. There were no bullet wounds and no blood dripping from his body so it was safe to assume he'd been hung up there while he was alive.

All together there were nine men scattered about the room. All were dead. The factory was a meeting point where a transaction involving fifteen kilos was supposed to take place. Obviously the men had been ambushed, robbed, and a whole lot worse.

Luke made his way to the man bent over the table. When he reached him, he stared at him for a moment. The side of the dead man's head lay flat on the table with his eyes open. Those eyes were now staring directly into Luke's. Luke didn't say a word. He just let his own eyes begin to survey the long knife inflicted gash that ran across the man's throat from his right ear to his left. Blood was spilling from it to the table. It was pooling underneath the man's upper body and dripping heavily to the floor gathering in a small pool that was gradually spreading.

"Muthafuckas!" Darien yelled angrily as he walked across the floor surveying the damage. "Muthafuckin' cock

34

suckers!"

Luke didn't let his eyes or attention leave the man on the table. He recognized him. That said a lot. The family's organization, especially its gunmen, runners and all those who did the dirty work, was a huge one. There were countless faces, some went just as quickly as they came and they were all expendable. *This* one though, Luke remembered. The man was in his early twenties. He'd seen Luke out somewhere and asked him for a job personally. He'd said he had been out of the penitentiary for several months and wasn't having any luck finding a job. He'd also said his fiancé was expecting their first child. Not truly giving him a second look, Luke simply gave him a number to a low level associate and kept it moving. Now though, Luke was definitely giving the man a second look.

Luke found himself bothered at the moment. He realized he didn't even know this man's name, a man who worked for him, a man whose job it was to place his freedom and life on the line for him. But the realization that gripped Luke the most was knowing that crossing paths with this man had cost him his life. It had cost a child their father. Allowing his hand to swipe his bald head, he joined his brother's rant about retaliation.

"Them sons of bitches gon' pay for this shit!" Luke yelled. He was beyond pissed off. "I swear they gon' pay!"

Luke finally walked away from the dead man who'd just captivated his thoughts. His face though and the gash across his throat was etched inside Luke's head.

Beginning to survey each man, Luke walked over them stepping in their blood and leaving a trail of bloody shoe prints behind himself. As his eyes took in everything, the sight was nothing new to him. It wasn't like he hadn't seen stuff like this before. He'd seen it countless times. It was a part of the business. This time though, it seemed different. It felt different.

Just like in the car watching over the battered body of the woman he loved, Luke was now second guessing his life and his profession. He'd been doing that a lot lately. The game had never bothered him up until the past few months. He didn't quite know why. He just knew he was developing a conscience. He was developing compassion. He was becoming something neither the game nor his own father had raised him to be…

Civilized.

Mr. Bishop had raised his sons in the underworld. He'd taught them to kill and how to become wealthy no matter the circumstance. He'd taught them the menacing ropes of running a crime family, especially during their teenage years. Yet most had no idea of some of the values he'd instilled in them that Luke was totally against then and now.

Luckily for Luke, after his death, he passed the reins over to them and their mother, allowing Luke more freedom to stray away from some of the disturbing ways their father truly believed in. Luke had been proud at that moment to carry on the family legacy. He'd been proud to finally play a part in expanding the family business. These days though, that feeling was fading.

As Luke now approached a young man lying on the floor, the first thing he noticed was that the young man's pants were down and he was clutching his crotch. Blood spilled from underneath his hands. As Luke neared him, he saw that the man's body seemed to be trembling.

He was still alive.

Luke rushed to him. When he reached him though, his heart sunk to his stomach. Just like the man bent over the table, Luke recognized this man, or rather this young boy. He was only seventeen. His name was Gavin.

Filthy Rich BY: KENDALL BANKS

He was Luke and Darien's nephew.

The two brothers had a sister named Trinity. She'd walked away from the family long ago, not wanting any parts of its bloody legacy or its crooked business dealings. She'd even gone as far as to change her last name. The last time the two brothers and even their mother saw her was at their dad's funeral, four years ago.

Gavin, although forbidden by his mother to even associate with his uncles, eventually got in touch with Darien. He'd heard the stories in the streets of how ruthless and respected the family was. He wanted to be a part of it. He wanted to be a gangster just like the rappers he'd heard and seen in countless videos on BET but could never get a crew to take him seriously because of his slight deformity. Sadly, Gavin was born with muscular dystrophy but never allowed it to keep him from engaging in the activities he yearned; a life of crime mostly. Since his early teen years he'd kept in touch with his uncles, uncles who loved him dearly. So of course when the time came, Darien, behind Trinity's back and against Luke's wishes, gave him a job.

Now he was nearly dead.

Luke rushed to his nephew's aid. Gurgling and choking, Gavin lay on the floor with his own dick shoved deeply into his mouth. Blood oozed from several bullet wounds in his stomach and chest. Ripping the penis from his nephew's mouth and tossing it, Luke quickly knelt and took his nephew's head into his arms. "Darien!" he screamed.

"I…I…can't…" Gavin attempted as blood ran from his mouth down the sides of his face onto Luke's lap. His eyes were wide. His chest was heaving up and down underneath his T-shirt quickly.

"Darien!" Luke called again as he sat underneath his nephew's head holding him in his arms. His eyes quickly

37

darted up and down at his wounds taking in the bullet holes and pouring crimson liquid. He was almost in shock himself at the sight.

Darien rushed towards them. When he reached them, recognizing his nephew, his eyes grew wide. He shook his head in disbelief.

"Nooooooo!" Darien hollered, refusing to accept what he was seeing. "No," he said again. He just kept repeating that word over and over. "It can't be." He began pacing the floor while looking at his nephew. "Fuck!" he yelled. "Them muthafuckas gon' pay!" he shouted while throwing a metal object into a pole.

Luke began to rock back and forth while cradling his nephew's head. "You're gonna be alright, Gavin," he said knowing it wasn't true. He just hoped his words could somehow help Gavin through the moment. "We're gonna get you fixed up."

Looking up into his uncle's eyes, Gavin whispered, "I…I…can't feel…my…my…legs."

"You're gonna be okay," Luke assured him again.

"I can't…feel…feel them…Uncle…Uncle Luke."

Terror, pain, sadness, bewilderment and so many other expressions were on Gavin's young face as his eyes stayed locked on his Uncle's face. His body shook uncontrollably. "They…did…did… me bad."

"Don't speak, Gavin," Luke told him. "It's going to be okay. You're going to be back on your feet in no time."

"Unc, they… wanna… kill…you."

"Shhh," Luke told him.

Then…

Luke wasn't prepared for Gavin's next set of words…

"Kill me," Gavin said.

Luke stared at his nephew, not sure if his ears were

playing tricks on him. He was sure he hadn't heard his nephew correctly. He couldn't have.

"Kill...kill..kill me, Uncle Luke."

Luke realized he *had* heard him correctly. Hearing them the second time hit him like a brick. He didn't even know how to respond.

"Please...please...Uncle Luke...kill kill me."

Shaking his head, Luke said, "Stop talking like that."

"Look at me, Unc. Look...look at...at me. Look... at what they...did to me."

He coughed up blood. A moment later he began to cough up his insides. He gritted his teeth at the pain. Tears began to fall from the outer corners of his eyes and roll down the sides of his face.

Darien had stopped pacing. He was now standing silently and staring down at his nephew.

Continuing on, Gavin said, "They cut my manhood off, man." Hurt and shame on his face. He began to cry even worse than before. Amidst his tears, he said, "They cut my- f-u-c-k-i-n dick off." He hesitated then continued, "I can't live like that."

Luke looked up at Darien who'd he'd never seen shed a tear in life. He was now glossy-eyed. Neither brother spoke. Their eyes just glared into each other's. Luke then looked back down at his nephew.

"Unc, I can't feel my legs," Gavin told him. "They took my dick. I can't go through fucking life like this."

Luke squeezed his nephew's hand tightly.

"Kill me," Gavin begged. "Please don't make me suffer."

The gunmen had now gathered. They stood around their two generals as they watched their own flesh and blood beg to die. They all stood silent.

"Kill me, Uncle Luke," Gavin whispered with more tears falling from his eyes. "Shoot me. Allow me some type of honor."

"Shhhhhhhh," Luke told him as he placed his index finger to his own lips.

Gavin didn't say another word. He just continued to stare up at his uncle hoping he'd grant his wish. His body continued to tremble. His heart beat thumped loudly. The pain of the gunshots and his castration was growing more and more unbearable. He looked like a scared little boy; a little boy who hadn't been terrorizing the streets of D.C. just days before.

Luke placed his thumb and index finger over his nephew's eyes and shut them. He then softly kissed him on the forehead, savoring its taste on his lips for as long as he could. Slowly he slid out from underneath him while laying the back of his head softly on the floor. Now standing and looking his brother in the eyes, he extended his hand for his gun. Darien obliged him. He placed the gun in his brother's hand. Luke then looked down brokenheartedly at his dying nephew. As he did, he remembered the day Trinity had proudly told him she was pregnant. He remembered being at her side in the delivery room as she gave birth. He remembered holding Gavin in his arms for the very first time. Each of those moments tormented him.

Luke aimed the gun and cocked the slide of the barrel.

No one said a word.

All eyes were on Gavin.

Moments passed.

Finally…

CRACK!!!

CRACK!!!

CRACK!!!

40

Luke squeezed the trigger letting off three shots into his nephew's chest. Within a brief second, Gavin's breathing stopped and his body went completely still. A louder and more intense silence than before seemed to fall over the room. With no hesitation Luke gave the gun back to his brother and walked off.

"Wait 'till mom hears about this shit," Darien said following his brother. "Blood is fenna run all over these muthafuckin' streets. We're gonna kill all those niggas."

Luke ignored Darien. He headed down the stairs to the first floor.

"What do you think? Do you think we should hit their asses tonight, bruh?"

Luke didn't say a word. He headed out the door.

"Luke!"

Luke continued walking. He even walked right past Darien's car.

"Luke, what's up? Where you goin'?"

Luke turned to his brother. Looking him directly in the eyes, he said, "We're getting out of this game."

Dairen looked at him like he was crazy. "What?"

"We're getting out, Darien."

"What the fuck you mean?"

"We're exiting this business as soon as possible; the guns, drugs, prostitution, everything; all of it. We're getting out."

Darien was pissed. "What the fuck you mean? Nigga, you trippin'. That's our nephew in there."

"You're muthafuckin' right that's our nephew!!!!!" Luke roared back at his brother louder than Darien had ever heard him yell before. Luke rarely yelled. He never showed emotion. He never even cursed. This was a surprise to Darien.

"I just had to kill our sister's only child, Darien!"

Luke continued. "We just lost nine men. And that's just *tonight*. That doesn't include the men we've lost over the *years*!"

Darien didn't speak.

"Eventually one of those men are going to be *us*, Darien. One of these days it's going to be *us* lying on the floor with a bullet in our heads!"

"Then that's chance we have to take, Luke. When we took over the business the day dad died, that's what we signed the fuck on for!"

Luke shook his head, angry that his brother wasn't seeing things the way he was.

"*We're* the nightmares, Luke!" Darien shouted. "*We're* the boogiemen. We make *other* muthafuckas retire from the game. *We* do that. Since when the fuck did that shit get twisted?"

"Fuck that! Darien, we're getting the fuck out of this game. There are too many other opportunities out there for us to find success in. And most of them are legal. We're going to take advantage of them!"

"Sounds like a coward move to me. I mean think about it. You got niggas in these streets after you. Instead of takin' care of them you wanna run like a lil' bitch!"

Losing his cool, Luke charged his brother, snatched him by the collar of his wife beater and forced him backwards towards the Aston Martin. Slamming him onto the hood so hard the entire car rocked, he said angrily and through gritted teeth, "Don't you ever in your muthafuckin' life call me a coward again!"

Darien didn't say anything. From the hood of the car, he didn't quite know what to make of his brother. He'd never seen his brother like this before. He'd never seen him that furious.

Luke finally let go of his brother. Taking a step back

and calming himself, he said in a calmer tone than before, "Those men in there had families. They had people who loved them, Darien."

"They knew that comin' into this shit, Luke. You can't pick and choose what days you wanna be a gangsta. You either in or out." Darien shrugged his shoulders nonchalantly.

"It doesn't have to be this way, Darien. I mean this game is like a revolving door, a never ending cycle. They kill us. We kill them. They make a move on us. We make a move on them. They lose men. We lose men. When the fuck does it stop, Darien?"

Darien didn't answer.

"We retaliate, they're going to retaliate. And eventually you and me are going to be caught in the cross fire, little brother."

"That's just the way it is," Darien told him shrugging it off. "To whom much is given, much is required. Ain't that what you always say?"

Luke sighed. He knew there was no getting through to Darien. Shaking his head, he turned around and headed off into the night.

"Where you goin'?" Darien shouted to him.

"For a walk!" Luke shouted over his shoulder.

"How you gon' get home?"

No answer.

"It's dangerous out there, nigga. Did you forget some very dangerous people want you dead?" he shouted.

Still no answer.

Darien said to a nearby soldier, "Follow him." Despite he and his brother's confrontation and difference of opinion, Darien still needed to be sure his brother was safe.

Dear Diary

Things getting real crazy. It's hard to trust anybody these days; especially bitches. First she told me she'd handle things then she told me to wait a little longer…now the bitch is ignoring my calls. One fact is for sure. I never had a problem murking a muthafucka. Shit's about to get **REAL.**

Filthy Rich BY: KENDALL BANKS

Chapter 5

The leather seats of the brand new white Bentley Wrath were unique leather and super soft. The dark tint of the windows casted a dark shadow over the entire interior. The dashboard's digital array of speedometers, stereo system, gave off a bluish glow, and the engine growled loudly each time Nessa's nude Giuseppe Zanotti pump pressed down on the gas pedal even in the least.

Dressed casually in a long, fashionable Helmut Lang tee, ripped jeans and Chanel sunglasses that hid her black eyes, Nessa leaned back into the driver's seat of the three hundred thousand dollar car as its air conditioning blew cool air from the dashboard vents. Her eyes were on the sunny highway ahead of her, but her mind wasn't. It was in deep thought and worry.

Sitting beside Nessa was her home-girl, Sidra. The two had been friends since their freshman year at Anacostia Senior High School. They'd been inseparable ever since.

"You alright?" Sidra asked.

Nessa didn't answer as the speeding cars on Suitland Parkway passed by her window. Nessa even found herself taking quick glances of the ocean blue sky. It was a beautiful summer day. She hadn't even heard her friend. Her mind was too focused on locating Luke.

"Nessa!" Sidra called out.

"What's up?" Nessa finally responded.

"I don't know. You tell me. I've been over here running my mouth like a dog race to your ass for the past fifteen minutes and you haven't said a damn word. You haven't even looked at me. What's going on?"

Nessa shook her head and told her, "Sorry, girl. Just got my mind on a lot of shit right now."

"Like what?"

"Just stuff."

Sidra nodded then twisted her lips into a nasty funk. "It's Luke, right?"

Nessa simply shook her head.

"Men do that shit to you. All of them fuckas."

"Being with him is starting to stress me the fuck out."

Looking at her friend like she'd lost her mind, Sidra asked, "Stressing you? Bitch, are you crazy? What the fuck do you have to be stressed about?"

"A lot. I can't…" Nessa paused to choose her words wisely. She knew the rules of the Bishop family. No one could be trusted and no one needed to know even the tiniest detail about their personal business.

"What? Say it…" Sidra urged.

"It's nothing. Just forget about it."

Nessa chuckled at her friend's crazy looking facial expression.

"Bitch, you livin' in a mansion out in Potomac, Maryland while most of the niggas I fuck wit' ain't never been out of Southeast. You drive the baddest fuckin' whip in town, and got a slew of choices in Luke's six car garage.

47

Andddddddd…you're rockin' the baddest shoes and clothes."

Nessa's mind refocused. She thought of her designer wardrobe. The one filled with clothes that every girl wanted to have and the one with countless pairs of Louboutins, Valentino's and Gucci's. Not to mention, her handbag collection would even make a basketball wife jealous. From Celine, Louis Vuitton to YSL and Hermes…Nessa had it all.

"Shiiittt…your ass always look good. I gained at least fifteen pounds since the last time I've seen you," Sidra added. "I mean do you remember how fine I was in high school? I used to have a bad ass body like Kim Kardashian." Sidra quickly looked into the sun visor's mirror. "And I gotta get this ratchet-ass weave done, too," she said, studying her ombre colored weave. "I need a total fuckin' makeover."

Sidra's rambling brought Nessa back to reality. "And let me add, you have one of the finest niggas in the DMV area. Bitch please, what the hell are you trippin' about? Work the game. Don't let the game work you."

Nessa shrugged her shoulders and took a hand off the wheel to push her sunglasses further onto her face.

Looking out of her own window, Sidra added, "That's a long way from the damn Barry Farm, boo boo I'll tell you that. You came up. You found a way out. Don't let the small shit get to you."

Nessa thought deeply about her friend's words. Secretly, she missed the hood at times. She missed the drama. She missed the noise. The suburbs were too stiff and quiet. She never truly felt comfortable. That's why she came back Southeast and swooped up Sidra on the regular. She knew fucking with Luke was a come up though.

"And Nessa, you need to make that nigga know that

even though chicks are thirsty and love a chocolate nigga with a bald head, he not gon' keep hittin' you."

Nessa damn near froze.

Silence filled the car.

"What do you mean?"

"I mean you think I can't see the bruises? Look at your damn fingers. Your fuckin' nails are gone. It looks like you were fightin' for your life. That nigga must be on some cave-man shit."

Nessa quickly looked over at her childhood friend as she shook her head. "It's not like that Sidra," she fired back. "It's too complicated. But just know he doesn't beat me."

"Oh, so that makes you a GIGANTIC punk, cause the only other explanation is that you let some bitch beat your ass."

"Sidra, forget about all that. You'll know when I'm ready for you to know. My biggest problem right now is Luke's mother. She's not making living with them easy on me," Nessa whined as she whipped a sharp curve.

"Well, just to put the shit out there, I think it's weird as hell that Luke lives with his mother anyway. I mean, I know it's a big ass house, but that's just odd. And his brother lives there too, right?"

Nessa nodded. "Yeah."

"See…somethin' ain't right about that shit."

"Yeah, when I first moved in I thought so, too. His brother doesn't bother me, he's out of the house most times,but his mother is a straight up, bitch! Every time I look around, she's eyeing me up and down all crazy and shit. She's always looking for a damn reason to fuck with me. She's got a real problem with me being with Luke. I don't know what the fuck is wrong with her."

"Fuck her. Who are you supposed to be making

happy? Her or her damn son?"

"You're right. I feel you but damn."

"But damn *what*? You lookin' for her approval? Shit, if she's not tryin' to give it to you, fuck her. Luke is what matters."

"She threatened my life."

"What?"

Nessa nodded. "You heard me correctly. The bitch threatened my fucking life."

"Well, did you whoop her muthafuckin' ass?" Sidra questioned.

They both laughed.

Nessa held the side of her hip. "Please don't make me laugh. I'm so damn sore."

"So, you still not gonna tell me what happened, huh?"

"It's nothing, Sidra. Trust me."

"Well, anyway you need to kick that old ladies ass the next time she bothers you."

"You know I can't do that. I wanted to give her a quick jab to her little pointy ass face, but that's Luke's mother. I had to hold myself back."

"Fuck that shit. When a person's life is threatened, all bets are off. She thinks she can't get her head bussed wide the fuck open 'cause she's rich."

"All that *sounds* good. And of course, where you and me come from, a bitch gets dealt with for making those type of threats. But this situation is a little different."

"How is it different?"

"It just is. I have to handle it in a special kind of way."

"How?"

Don't worry. I'm going to handle it."

"How?" Sidra asked once again. She was the type

of chick who rolled her neck and poked out her lips between words. "I hope you don't handle it the same way you
did when you earned those war marks on your face.

"In my own way. I got it."

"Well, how did Luke feel about her threatenin'
you?"

"Haven't told him yet?"

Nessa changed lanes.

"Why the fuck not?" Sidra barked and smacked her
lips all at the same time. "Uggghhhh."

"Haven't spoken to him since the night it happened.
That was a couple of nights ago. Haven't seen him.
Haven't even heard from him. That's another thing that's
got my head fucked up right now."

Nessa sped up and made the vehicle hit eighty-five
after noticing two guys in a nearby Cadillac CTS trying to
get her attention.

"Do you think something's wrong?"

"I don't know what to think, Sidra. My mind is
fucked up right now."

"You called him?"

"Of course. Texted him, too. No answer. No response." Nessa could sense that Sidra would keep digging
so she tried to end things even though she was worried as
hell about Luke. The death toll in the city had been increas-
ing by the hour so since Luke was a target, there was a
strong possibility she would never see him again. "His
brother said he's fine. He just needs some space."

"Space means he's fuckin' a bitch on the side. You
know that, Nessa. Stop actin' like you just came off the
porch. If you need me to go with you to roll up on a bitch,
just let me know."

"Everything's good, Sidra. Don't worry about it."

Suddenly Nessa's phone rang. While keeping one

hand on the steering wheel, she reached behind her seat into her purse and pulled out her phone. Glancing at the screen and seeing the number, she shook her head and raised her eyes back to the windshield. The number belonged to her father and she didn't want to talk to him right now. Pressing the end button and dropping the phone in her lap, his call brought back memories, memories she wasn't sure how she felt about, memories she wasn't sure if she should be leaving behind, or carrying along with her. As she drove, one in particular appeared in her mind.

Nessa had just turned nine years old. It was the day of her birthday. The sun blazed beautifully as she and her father happily made their way about the crowded circus grounds. Leading up to that day, Nessa had been practically begging her father to take her to the circus. He promised. And just like always, he kept his promise.

Mr. Byron Kingston was dressed in a short-sleeved Polo shirt, and freshly creased shorts as expensive cologne radiated from his body. He was a handsome and tall muscular man who took immense pride in his appearance. You never caught him unshaven or shabbily dressed. When he walked, he strutted. Best believe, people paid attention.

As Nessa held her dad's hand while going on rides and playing countless games, she felt so proud to be his daughter and to be by his side. It meant the world to her. He was her Superman and she always felt like his princess.

Both Nessa and her father were just coming off of the Ferris Wheel when a young man jogged up to them and whispered something in Byron's ear. Nessa couldn't hear what was whispered as she stood beside her father in a white, fluffy dress.

"You sure?" Byron asked the young man in a serious tone.

The young man nodded.

Filthy Rich BY: KENDALL BANKS

Before Nessa knew it, without a reason why, she and her father were headed back to the parking lot. Seconds later, they were in his brand new black Lincoln Town Car and leaving.

"Where are we going?" Nessa asked, barely tall enough to see over the dashboard. Her feet weren't even long enough to touch the floor.

"Gotta handle some business, sweetheart," he said. "We'll come back later."

Nessa was disappointed but didn't say anything more.

The Lincoln pulled into the parking lot of a strip club fifteen minutes later. Shutting off the engine, Byron told Nessa, "Stay in the car." He then hopped out and closed the door.

Nessa placed her knees into the seat and looked over the dashboard to see her father walk across the parking lot and approach several men. For several moments they all spoke, but Nessa couldn't make out what they were saying. Clearly though, whatever was being discussed, she could tell by the angry look on her father's face it was something that had pissed him off. Nessa continued to watch. Several moments later, her eyes widened when she saw each man, including her father, pull guns from underneath their shirts. She then watched as they headed into the strip club.

Leaning back into her seat, Nessa wondered what was going on. She wondered why her father and his men needed guns. Up until that particular moment, Nessa had never seen a gun except on television.

As time passed, one minute turned to two. Two minutes turned to several. Nessa grew impatient. But more importantly, just like any other nine year old child, she grew more and more inquisitive. She wanted to know what was

53

going on. She had to know. So, although her father had told her to stay in the car, she got out anyway and headed across the lot. As she walked, the heels of her shoes clicked loudly. Seconds later, she reached the door, opened it and walked inside. Underneath dim lights, immediately she smelled cigarette smoke as she passed the bouncer's chair, which was empty. She also heard yelling and cursing. A short distance later, she saw a stage with a pole in the center of it. Afterward, her eyes came across a situation obviously no nine year old child should see...

Throughout the club, naked women laid sprawled out on the floor on their stomachs with their arms outstretched. Several men were also laid out. Over each of them stood the men who'd been outside conversing with her father. Their guns were pointed at each man and woman. As they were, some of the women were crying while others begged for their lives. Across the floor of the club, Nessa could hear her father's voice. There was anger in it.

Suddenly...

One of the gunmen abruptly turned to Nessa and pointed his gun at her. Caught off guard by her presence, he said, "What the fuck?"

Nessa froze in her tracks. Her eyes locked on the gun. She didn't know what to do. The other gunmen, while still keeping their guns trained on the people lying at their feet, also turned to Nessa. She was immediately scared.

"Yo, Byron!" one of the gunmen called.

Byron, with his gun pointed at the head of a man kneeling in front of him, turned around. Seeing his daughter, he said, "She's good. Come here, sweetheart."

Nessa didn't move. The entire scene scared her. She now wished she had stayed in the car like she had been told.

Filthy Rich BY: KENDALL BANKS

"It's okay, baby," Her father told her. "No one's gonna hurt you. Come here."

Nessa walked throughout the maze of pointed guns and sprawled out bodies directly to her father as fast as she could. As she did, she could see the fear and tears in each of the women's eyes. She didn't quite know what to make of it.

"Didn't I tell you to stay in the car?" Nessa's father told her when she reached him.

She nodded innocently.

Shaking his head, he said, "Well, what's done is done. We'll deal with it later."

As Nessa stood directly by her father's side, his attention went back to the man kneeling in front of him. The man was crying as he looked up at Byron with terror in his eyes.

With the gun pointed at the man's head, Byron asked his daughter, "Sweetheart, you see this man right here?"

Nessa nodded.

"He did a bad thing."

"What did he do?" she asked in a soft, delicate voice.

"He borrowed some money from me, a whole lot of money. Fifty thousand dollars to be exact. Then when it came time to pay it back, he went missing."

"Byron," the man said quickly. "I swear I wasn't hiding. I was going to get you your money. I was going..."

"Shut the fuck up!" Byron roared.

The cowering man did as he was told.

Nessa's body tensed. She'd never heard her father yell before.

"You borrowed that money six muthafuckin' months ago!" Byron continued. "We've been everywhere lookin' for your ass ever since. Haven't found you anywhere. The last

55

Filthy Rich BY: KENDALL BANKS

I heard, your ass skipped town; went down to Detroit. Now, your snake ass done slithered back into town thinkin' me and my people weren't going to see you."

"Byron, I'm gonna get your money."

"Too late."

"But…"

"Shut the fuck up!"

The man dropped his head and began whimpering like a baby. He knew death was only moments away. If not death, at least something that would make him wish for death.

Speaking to his daughter again, Byron asked, "Baby, when someone does wrong, what happens?"

"They get a punishment," she answered innocently.

"Right."

The man whimpered even harder and even more loudly at the sound of those words. Sweat ran from his forehead and soaked his shirt.

"What do you think his punishment should be?" Byron asked.

"I don't know?" Nessa answered. She had no idea how to punish adults. Up until that point, she didn't even know adults received punishments.

"I think I should kill him."

"Oh God, please nooooooo," the man begged and pleaded.

"What do you think, baby?"

Nessa shook her head quickly and said, "No, daddy." Although a child, she knew what death was. She knew there was no coming back from it.

"You don't think he should die?"

"No, daddy, don't."

Byron chuckled. "The naivety of a child," he said. Then without warning…

56

Filthy Rich BY: KENDALL BANKS

Gun shots rang out. The gun roared loudly in Nessa's ears. Byron had squeezed the trigger. The bullet of the .45 Magnum revolver tore through the kneeling man's forehead with so much force and power it ripped his face in half. The demolition of flesh kicked back blood into Nessa's face and all over her white dress as the man's body collapsed to the floor with half his face gone and his brains splattered on the floor underneath his back.

Nessa's ears continued to ring. Her body trembled. Her eyes were on the man's dead body as blood poured from what used to be his head. It ran from his destroyed skull like water from a spilled mop bucket. The sight along with the stench radiating from the blood she was now covered with disgusted her but yet she couldn't turn her eyes away. She couldn't stop looking.

"I'm not a muthafuckin' game!" Byron yelled to everyone around him. "If you owe me, pay me!"

That was the very first time Nessa had witnessed her father kill anyone. It wasn't the last though. She personally witnessed murder and other business dealings of his numerous times throughout her childhood until the Feds finally had enough on him to destroy his enterprise. It wasn't like Nessa had her mother to run to. She'd gone missing at that time landing Nessa in the custody of Children's Services at the defenseless age of 12.

Now once again paying attention to the highway in front of her, Nessa had mixed thoughts and feelings about her father. She didn't know whether to love him or hate him. All she knew was it was him who had planted the seed in her that dictated she be a queen of these streets no matter what it took. She wanted everything he once had and then some.

Moments later, Sidra's voice brought Nessa back to reality. "You hear me, girl? Your phone is goin' off like crazy."

Nessa looked down and realized her cell was alerting her about text messages coming in. She assumed it was her father. Strangely, it wasn't.

Oh, so you ignoring me, now? Really Bitch? Really?

You think shit's a game…but I WILL kill you, too.

Filthy Rich BY: KENDALL BANKS

Chapter 6

The bedroom was huge, much bigger than the average. It was furnished scarcely though with only a bed, dresser and chair. Its floor was bare, no carpet. Its windows, although tall, were each covered with bars that stretched from the top of the windows to the bottom. There was also a large bathroom connected to the bedroom.

In the center of the room was a large, high back chair, fit for a king. Sitting in that chair was a black man in his thirties. He was dressed in a pair of pajamas and house shoes. His hair was a thick and heavily matted afro that hadn't been cut or cared for in years. Along his face was a beard that was just as matted as the afro. The man's body was covered in scabs from lack of bathing. His pores and clothes also reeked heavily of urine.

It was now about four o'clock in the afternoon as the man sat staring out of the window uttering not a single word. As a drenching rain poured outside the window and occasional cracks of thunder and lightning rumbled across the sky outside, he watched without blinking. In fact, it was as if although staring at the rain and lightning, he was seeing *through* it, far beyond it.

The man's body hadn't moved in hours. The air conditioning was cool but didn't seem to faze him. He sat absolutely still. Besides the rise and fall of his stomach as he breathed, the only movement coming from him was the thick strands of saliva stretching sloppily from the corner of his mouth down his beard and into the lap of his urine drenched pajamas.

The bedroom itself was the man's entire world. It was his entire universe. For the past four years, it had been all he'd ever known. He'd never been outside it not even for a second. He hadn't even stepped even a single toe outside its door. The windows were his only connection to the world outside it.

Thunder rolled.

The knob of the bedroom door turned.

The door opened.

A woman appeared, one of power, money, and respect. Behind her were two tall and solidly muscular men dressed in black suits. Both of them held guns at their sides as they escorted the woman inside. As they made an attempt to escort the woman across the room towards the man in the chair, she signaled that their assistance wouldn't be necessary. Their menacing presence in the room was enough. Reaching the man in the chair, her nose and face cringed at the stench of urine. Covering her nose, she told him, "You reek."

He didn't say anyhing. He didn't even look at her. He just continued to stare out of the window in front of him.

"I provide you with a bathroom," she continued. "Your dresser is filled with clothes. But you're too damn sorry to even use the toilet, take a shower or change clothes?"

Still…

Filthy Rich BY: KENDALL BANKS

No answer.

Blocking his view of the window, the woman took the man's chin into her hand forcefully, raised his eyes to her and screamed, "You hear me talking to you!"

SMACK!!!!!

The sound of her hand colliding with his face echoed throughout the room. As it did, both men in suits held tighter to their guns. Their fingers locked tightly around the triggers.

"When I speak to you, you answer me, damn it!" she screamed.

Instead of answering the old woman directly, the man in the chair just began to rock back and forth and talk to himself. His speech couldn't be understood. It sounded more like babble.

"Simple minded bastard," she spewed at him.

He just continued his babbling.

Letting go of his chin, she pulled two pills from the pocket of her dress. She held them in front of his eyes. For the first time in hours, his attention focused on something besides the window and the rain. A glimmer appeared after being asked, "Are these what you want?"

He nodded.

"You sure?'

He nodded again.

"Well, you know the deal. I have to get what I want first."

Displeasure appeared on his face.

"Awwwwww," she mocked him. "I guess you don't want your medication then."

He nodded. He wanted the pills. They were just as important to him as the room itself. They were the only thing that got him through the countless lonely night and days. He *needed* them.

62

Smiling at his nodding, she said, "Then get on your job." She then raised her dress to expose her pantyless pussy while raising a foot onto the arm of the chair.

The man hesitated.

SMACK!!!!!

"Eat!" the woman yelled as she slapped him across the face.

After a brief hesitation more, he did as he was told. He buried his face in her crotch and began to lap up her juices.

"That's a good boy," she told him as she placed a hand to the back of his head and forced his face to remain where she wanted it.

The man licked and slurped.

The two gunmen had seen this scene countless times over the past four years. It was nothing new to them. Knowing it had pretty much become a part of their jobs, they just stood by and looked on.

The woman moaned and groaned while raising her face to the ceiling and closing her eyes. With a hand in the man's afro, she moaned, "Eat that pussy, nigga. Eat it good for me."

Without hesitation, the man did as he was told.

"Work the clit."

He did. His tongue swirled around it over and over again while he occasionally sucked softly on it.

"Yes, baby, work that clit."

He continued to do as he was told.

"Ahhhhhhhhh…yesssssssss…right there..." She moaned in ecstasy.

The woman began to buck like a horse allowing her pelvis to slip into a possessed state.

"Don't stop, muthufucka! I dare you!" she screamed. "Ooooooooooohhhh," she chanted while allowing herself to drool.

Moments passed. As they did, the woman's body endured pleasures and ecstasies that she didn't receive often. She loved it, especially the feeling of dominance she had over the man. There was nothing like making a man do what she wanted him to, especially a man who had once been entitled to a powerful empire, an empire *she* had taken away from him.

"Eat it faster," she ordered.

His mouth and tongue made lapping sounds like a dog drinking water from a bowl. The sounds had even caused the tall guards' dick to harden even though he was now facing the opposite direction.

"Ahhhhhhhhh shit," she sounded.

Finally.

She came. She exploded into his mouth so hard her knees buckled. Grabbing a tighter grip on his afro, she smeared her juices into his face until they covered his beard. Finally, backing away and dropping her dress, she smirked down at him and said, "That was weak, nowhere near as good as the last time. I shouldn't reward you."

He dropped his head in shame.

Smiling, the old woman dropped the pills to the floor. As soon as she did, he lunged from his chair to the floor and grabbed them. Immediately after, he shoved them in his mouth and swallowed.

Shaking her head, she said, "Pitiful."

He rocked back and forth on the floor as the pills immediately began to take effect. It didn't matter to him that they turned his brains to mush. All he cared about was the high.

The menacing woman nodded to the gunmen. They then approached. As they did, one pulled a syringe from his pocket. Seeing the men approach and seeing the syringe, the man's eyes grew wide. He shook his head and began to back towards the nearest wall while on his butt.

"Don't make this harder than it has to be," the old woman told him.

He shook his head upon reaching the wall. He loved taking the pills but he hated the syringe. The men were now towering over him. Seconds later, a struggle ensued. When it was done, the man was lying on his stomach screaming as both men straddled his body and held him down. A moment later, the needle of the syringe was stuck into his arm. As he struggled, the needle's contents spewed into his veins.

Finally…

He fell still, his eyes glossy and staring into space.

The gunmen stood and headed back to the door.

The old woman stared at the man as he now lay on his stomach curling into a fetal position like a child. She then headed to the door. Reaching it, she turned to give him one final look. Displeased with what she saw, she said to him, "And to think you were once the heir to an empire."

Shaking her head, she and her henchmen walked out of the room and locked the door.

Chapter 7

Nessa's ringing phone startled her.

She grabbed it quickly, hoping it was Luke. To her surprise it wasn't the call she'd wanted.

The voice was chilling.

Menacing.

Violent.

It's raspy sound caused goosebumps to appear all over Nessa's arms. Then she spoke.

"Bitch, don't play with me," the woman fired. "Now, I've been patient enough. Come through like you said you would or I'll show up at the Bishop home and kill you right in front all them sons a bitches!" She paused with a loud, thunderous laugh. "And then you won't have to worry about your cover being blown."

"Look…" Nessa started to say.

The line went completely dead. Before Nessa could collect her thoughts, the phone rang again. This time she recognized the number.

"What is it, dad?" Nessa answered aggravated as she leaned against the kitchen island. Her father had been ringing her phone over and over again nonstop.

"That's how you answer a phone?" he asked with disapproval. "That's how you greet your old man? Well, damn."

"Dad, I'm busy," she lied. Her tone made it clear she just didn't want to talk to him.

"Since when did you become too busy for your father?"

She rolled her eyes.

"Since when did that start? Hell, we two of a kind, right?"

"Dad, what do you want? How much do you need?" Nessa knew there was a reason behind the call, an ulterior motive. Her father never called unless he wanted something, usually money or to be bailed out of jail.

"Nooooo, I don't need money," he said chuckling. "Why would you ask that?"

"Because that's usually what you want."

"Well no, I don't need money."

She sighed knowing whatever her father wanted, he was attempting to butter her up real good. She knew him like a book.

"Can't a father just call to talk to his little girl?"

"Dad, cut the damn act. Tell me what you want or I'm hanging up the damn phone."

"Alright, alright," he said quickly. "Don't hang up."

"Then what do you want."

"I need to talk to you about something."

"About what?"

"Something important."

"Okay, what is it?"

"Not over the phone. Want to talk to you face to face. It's very important."

Not wanting to see him, she sighed and said, "Dad, I don't think that would be a good…"

"Baby, please," he begged, cutting her off. "It's important. I won't take too much of your time. I promise. Besides, I miss seeing my little girl's face. Please, Nessa?"

She didn't answer. Her mind kept drifting back to Luke. He hadn't been home or even called her in the past two days. Although the family told her not to worry, she'd heard that a few bodies had been found in an area of Northeast where Luke frequently hung out. Unfortunately for Luke, he'd ditched his bodyguards a day ago saying he wanted to be alone. Now, the entire family was on edge.

"It would mean a lot to me, sweetie."

Her father's voice snapped her back to reality.

She gave in reluctantly feeling sorry for him. "Where?"

"Tomorrow…at Haines Point, where I used to take you to when you were a little girl. Tomorrow morning. Ten o'clock."

"It's not Haines Point anymore, dad. They changed the name to East Potomac or something like that."

"Well shit, Nessa who cares? Just meet me there."

"Alright. I'll be there but won't stay long."

"Thank you, princess. I love…"

"Gotta go," she told him and ended the call before he could finish his sentence. She continued leaning against the island staring out of the picture window across the vast lakefront property to the crashing waves of the lake itself. She wondered what her father wanted. At the same time though, she wasn't interested. She figured it could be another one of his damn get rich quick schemes.

Refusing to give her father any more space in her head, Nessa finally left the kitchen. As she entered the foyer, she saw Luke's mother, Darien and another man talking. The man's name was Brandon Bishop. He was a chocolate, tall, square jawed, square shouldered man with one deep dimple in his left cheek and way too much swag. He was handsome with big brown eyes and always wore nice, tailor-made suits; totally the opposite of Darien who was dressed in a white-T, Gucci high-top sneakers, and jeans that hung below his ass.

Besides being a cousin, Nessa didn't know exactly what Brandon's position was in the family business. She knew whatever it was though, it must've been important because he came by often. As Nessa entered the foyer, she looked at Brandon quickly from head to toe. She couldn't help it. She didn't allow it to be an obvious fawning sort of look though. She was with Luke, of course. Still, just like any other time Brandon came by, she snuck in a look nevertheless.

Brandon looked over Chetti's shoulder and spotted Nessa. A smile slipped through his clinched lips instantly. He ended his part of the conversation and signaled to everyone they had company. All words ceased as Chetti turned around and saw Nessa standing there. Spite and contempt immediately filled her eyes and expression.

"Damn, bitch," she said. "Didn't anyone ever teach you to *announce* yourself when you walk into an occupied room of someone's home?"

Before Nessa could answer, Chetti shook her head, turned back to both Brandon and her son and said, "Allow a stray into your house and they begin to think they own the place."

Nessa rolled her eyes behind Chetti's head. As she did, Brandon's eyes surveyed her body as quickly and slyly as hers had done him. Even with bruises still evident, she looked amazing. With a tight body and all the right curves, Brandon understood why Luke allowed her into his space.

Nessa took her eyes off of Chetti in time to notice Brandon's stare. Feeling uneasy, she changed the subject quickly. "Has anyone heard from Luke?" she asked with worry in her voice.

"No," Chetti snapped. "And when we do, you'll be the last to know."

"Ma, cut that shit out," Darien fired, running his hands through his freshly done dreads.

"Why! She might be the reason he's missing. I mean we barely know this tramp. Luke's only been dealing with her for a year, and you can never trust a bitch with long-ass weave."

"A year and a half," Nessa quickly corrected.

"Ummm huh. Bitch, whatever."

It took every bone in Nessa's body not to say anything back. She was from the streets and would sweep the floor with Chetti's ass if she wanted to. But staying true to the game, she knew her mission would be interrupted if she challenged Chetti. "Stay the course," Nessa told herself under her breath.

"Nessa, don't worry," Darien consoled her. "He's just being stubborn. We'll find him. I know you really love my bro."

"We're talking business," Chetti told Nessa without bothering to turn to her again. "*Family* business, mind you. Make your ass scarce." With her hand she made a shoeing motion over her shoulder to Nessa like a person swatting away a fly.

All of a sudden, the door of the foyer opened. Nessa's eyes widened when she saw Luke appear. "Baby!" she yelled, rushing into his arms. The two kissed deeply. Despite being in a slight bit of pain, Nessa gave him a huge hug. When they released each other, she asked, "Where have you been? You had me worried. I didn't know if you were dead or alive!"

"Had some things on my mind."

Filthy Rich BY: KENDALL BANKS

"Do you want to talk about it? And why didn't you call me?"

Before he could answer, Chetti brushed past Nessa knocking her back on her heels on purpose. "Nonsense," she said. "No time for petty discussion. We have business to discuss." She placed an arm underneath Luke's. Seconds later, they were headed beneath the grand double staircase to the den leaving Nessa behind. Once they reached it and walked inside, Chetti turned at the doorway, glared across the marble floor at Nessa, smirked and slammed the door.

The imported Italian mahogany table was long and freshly polished. The high-back chairs around it were mahogany and imported also. Along the walls were towering bookshelves filled with classical books by foreign authors. A Spanish rug covered most of the floor. At the far end of the table was a picture window that showcased the estate's massive grounds and breathtaking lakefront view. Boats could be seen riding the waves.

Chetti sat at the head of the table. While leaning back into her chair with her legs crossed, she said to Luke with sarcasm, "Glad to see you finally come out of hiding."

"I hide from no one, mother. You know that."

"I would've had more respect for you if I'd found out you were dead."

Luke sat on one side of the table. Brandon and Darien sat directly across from him on the other side. His face balled up into a knot thinking about his mother's comment.

"You'll attend my funeral someday, but now is not the time. I just needed to clear my head for a minute,"

Luke continued.

"Well, while you were clearing your fuckin' head, the streets are thinkin' we're soft," Darien told him.

Chetti nodded in agreement while sipping on a glass of tequila.

"Let 'em think what they want," Luke told his brother calmly.

"You know that's not an option," Chetti belted. "Not when their perception of us is that we're weak and running scared with our tails between our legs."

"Hell yeah," Darien said, moving his body in a jittery motion. "That's why it's time we hit them muthafuckas and hit 'em hard. Wipe their asses the fuck off the map."

Luke didn't respond. He didn't look at his brother because he hated the way he jumped around anxiously and never thought things out carefully. Luke simply dropped his eyes to the floor as if almost bored with the conversation.

"What do you know about them?" Chetti asked Brandon.

Brandon had been a Federal Agent for fifteen years. He was the family's number one key to longevity in the drug business. He was able to keep the FBI off their ass while also keeping Law Enforcement in the city off of them also.

Leaning forward and resting his forearms on the table's surface, Brandon said, "They're an organization out of Los Angeles, big fish. They're running the drug trade up there. They wiped out all major competition."

Chetti and Darien listened carefully.

"Over the past few years, they've been expanding," Brandon continued. "Nevada, Georgia, now here in D.C. Their MO in each state and city is the same: attack the big fish aggressively and without warning. It's been successful in each state they've established their presence in."

"And now they've got their eyes set on D.C.?" Chetti asked.

Brandon nodded.

"Fuck that!" Darien yelled angrily. "We ain't rollin' over for them muthafuckas. Should've stayed their asses over in L.A. We don't play that shit 'round here!"

Luke didn't say a word. If anything, he seemed detached from the situation. His mind seemed to be somewhere else.

"So, what's going on with the FEDS?" Chetti asked Brandon. "A crew that big and violent couldn't have been flying underneath your radar."

"We've had an open investigation on them for the last three years. We've even sent a few agents undercover. Can't get anything on them though. Anytime we get something on them that even *looks* like it may stick, witnesses either mysteriously vanish or mysteriously pick up amnesia."

"What about the undercover agents?" Darien questioned.

"Each has popped up dead," Brandon replied.

Silence.

Everyone was silently thinking the same thing. If this organization would kill FEDS, they were beyond vicious. They couldn't be taken lightly at all.

"We've got to wipe 'em out *now*," Darien belted.

Noticing from the beginning how detached from the conversation Luke was, Chetti finally asked him, "What do you think we should do?"

Looking her squarely in the eyes, he answered, "Get out the game."

"What is that?" Darien asked. "Some fuckin' kind

of strategy or somethin'?"

Luke shook his head. "No, no strategy."

"See, Ma," Darien told his mother. "That's the same crazy ass shit the nigga was talkin' 'bout the other night. I told you. The muthafucka done fell and hit his head on somethin'."

"I haven't fallen and hit my head on shit."

"You must've," Chetti told him. "Your father and I didn't build a five hundred million dollar family by turning and running like cowards whenever the fire gets too hot."

"Mother, when are we gonna stop this? When are we gonna stop repeating this cycle?"

"What are you talking about?" Chetti asked.

"I'm talking about isn't the dream of a parent supposed to be seeing her children and grandchildren take a different road than them? Building a better life for themselves?"

She eyed Luke carefully.

"You just lost a grandchild to this game," he continued. "Now your daughter has to grieve the death of her only son. But yet you're basically moving in a direction that will eventually groom all of our seeds for the same thing. When does it stop?"

She didn't answer.

"You just said yourself that this family has an estimated worth of five hundred million dollars. Well why are we still risking our lives out here in these streets? Why are we still taking chances that will eventually cause our demise?"

Shaking his head in disagreement, Darien said, "This nigga done gon' fuckin' crazy."

"So you're saying walk away from a multimillion dollar industry in this city that we helped build?" Chetti asked Luke.

"Yes."

"Not in this lifetime," she spat.

"Why?" Luke countered.

"Because it's not an option."

"Why isn't it an option?"

"Because I said so," Chetti fired back.

"Well, that's not good enough," Luke replied.

"What?"

"That's not a good enough reason."

Chetti cut her eyes at her son. She could smell confrontation. "What does that mean?"

"Mother, no disrespect but your, "Say So" is outdated."

"Excuse me?" Chetti leaned forward to be sure she was hearing her son absolutely correctly.

"Mother, I think it's time the family headed in a different direction."

"And what direction is that?" Darien asked.

"It's time we go corporate. It's time we go legit."

"So, you're saying let someone else move in our territory?" Chetti questioned.

"Let 'em have it. We've eaten enough. It's time to move on to bigger and better things," Luke answered.

"Nonsense."

"No, what *you're* speaking is nonsense."

"Excuse me?"

"Over the past few days, I've been in discussion with a few people. I've invested several million into some legitimate ventures. I'm sure they'll pay off."

Chetti's face twisted immediately. "Who gave you the authority to invest millions of the family's dollars without permission?"

"Thirty-three percent of this family's fortune is mine. I don't have to ask."

Chetti was furious. "You son of a bitch!" she yelled furiously. "And you don't own thirty three percent. Trinity signed off her interest and since Cedrick is now deceased I own his interest as his next of kin."

Darien and Luke gawked at her oddly followed by Luke simply shaking his head at her.

"Who cares, Mother? I invested the money anyway."

The sound of Chetti's hand slamming onto the table got everyone's attention. "Contrary to fuckin' popular belief around here, *I'm* head nigga in charge. *I've* got the biggest dick. Nothing moves unless *I* say so!"

Luke remained calm. "Your 'Say So' got Gavin killed. I refuse to take another loss like that. When dad died, you know who he really left in charge…but who cares about all of that right now. It's time I pulled rank."

Chetti leapt to her feet so quickly her chair slid out from underneath her and toppled to the floor. "Listen here, you spoiled rotten muthafucka!" she yelled while jabbing a finger towards Luke's face. "I run this family. I do. And if you can't accept that, your ass is free to leave! But nigga when you go, leave the Bishop name and everything behind!"

Everyone grew silent.

Neither of the sons had ever challenged their mother's authority. It had always been a silent and unwritten rule that she was the leader. Now that the winds of change seemed to be blowing, the atmosphere of the room was a tense one.

"Mother, I was hoping you'd be reasonable about this," Luke said.

"Fuck you!" Chetti screamed.

Luke sighed. "Your call, Mother." He backed his chair from the table. "I'm accepting your offer to leave.

But my thirty three percent of the family and its interests come with me." He headed alongside the table towards the door.

Chetti stood there fuming.

Neither Darien nor Brandon said anything.

Suddenly as Luke nearly reached the door, Chetti darted toward him screaming dramatically, "Luke, baby, I'm sorry!" When she reached him, she grabbed his shoulder, turned him around and took his face into her hands while pressing his back flat against the wall. "I said things I didn't mean, sweetie." Her words were falling from her mouth fast and desperately. "Baby, don't leave."

Luke didn't speak.

His frown was of disgust.

"You know since your father died, you and Darien have been my men." She took her son in her arms and placed her breasts tightly against his chest. She then began to plant kisses all over his face. "You can't leave, baby."

Brandon watched from his chair. The way Chetti engaged with her son didn't seem appropriate. She caressed and rubbed him as if he were her man. Brandon didn't say anything though. He glanced over at Darien and noticed that he didn't even seem fazed. He wondered how much Darien had actually witnessed before. He'd heard the family stories. He knew of the hushed secrets forbidden to ever be discussed. Still, it all shocked him.

"I'm so sorry, baby," she continued. She then kissed Luke in the mouth deeply and passionately. She slipped her tongue into his mouth and held him tightly.

Quickly pulling away from his mother, Luke opened the door and attempted to walk out of the den.

Keeping grip of him and attempting to kiss him again, Chetti pleaded, "Luke, wait."

He snatched away from her and headed for the front

door. As he did, she fell to the floor screaming with tears in her eyes, "Baby, I love you. You and Darien are my favorite men. Luke don't leave me!"

Luke opened the door, walked out of the house and slammed the door behind him.

"Luke!" she screamed while reaching for him from the floor although he was now gone.

Both Darien and Brandon helped Chetti to her feet. She looked like a savage. Her hair was covering her face wildly. Her eyes were red and wide. She was crying so hard, saliva drooled from her mouth and strands of snot were dripping from her nostrils. Immediately, she grabbed hold of Darien as if her life depended on it refusing to let him go. With tears pouring down her face and fear in her eyes, she begged, "Baby, tell mommy you love her."

"I love you, Ma," Darien said with concern for his mother's mental health.

Planting kisses all over his face, she pleaded, "Promise me, baby."

"I promise."

"Tell me you'll never leave your mommy." Her eyes searched his face for each answer with eager and desperate anticipation before he could open his mouth.

"I'll never leave you, Ma."

Then just as she'd done to Luke, she slipped her tongue into Darien's mouth. Uncomfortable with the sight, Brandon turned away. He headed back into the den and sat down.

"Get yourself together, Ma," Darien whispered to her. "We've got to figure out what we're going to do about this situation."

She turned and looked at the front door with an obviously broken heart. "Do you think Luke will come back?"

"Of course, Ma. He just needs to cool down."

An evil expression enveloped her face. "I know what it is. I know exactly what the problem is."

"What, Ma?"

Looking towards the ceiling, she said, "It's that bitch. It's that ghetto-trash-ass bitch. She's turning my son against me."

Ushering his mother back to the den, Darien said, "Come on, Ma."

Panic then filled her face. "Do you think he loves her more than me?"

"Of course not, Ma."

"Is he taking her away from me?"

"No, Ma. She's just a freak."

"I'm his favorite, aren't I?"

"Yes, Ma."

"You hoodrat whore!" Chetti screamed as she was escorted back to the den hoping Nessa could hear her. "You'll never have my son. I'll never let you have him. You'll never turn him against me. You'd better hear me, bitch!"

Darien finally managed to pull his mom in the den and shut the door. Seconds later, a nearby door opened. Nessa emerged. She'd definitely heard Chetti just as the old bitch had wished. Listening at the den's door earlier, she'd also heard everything else. She wasn't quite sure what she would do with everything she'd heard but she knew it would be useful with the plan she'd concocted.

For now, she needed to find Luke.

Chapter 8

Shortly after 8:00 a.m. Nessa's phone buzzed, waking her from her quick cat nap. The text message from Sidra was annoying, but she was glad that it had come through. Nessa had been up the entire night worried about Luke. She'd called him countless times only to keep getting his voice mail.

Quickly, Nessa responded to Sidra, sat up and tried Luke again. The sound of his voice shocked her.

"Luke?"

"Yeah."

"Where in the hell have you been?" she spat. "I've been worried like shit about you."

"I'm good," he said dryly.

"I would know that if you'd answered your fucking phone. I called all damn night! You telling me you didn't see my calls?"

"Nessa, look, this is the price you pay to be involved with a guy like me. Hell, I told you from the start."

"You didn't tell me shit from the start!" she fired.

Luke's words took Nessa back to the first time they met. For her, it was love at first sight when Luke walked

80

into the Jamaican restaurant on U Street. Nessa had been *kickin' it in the lobby area with a small level dope boy named Mook when a pair of green eyes caught her attention. They were the most exotic and hypnotizing set of eyes she'd ever seen. She was captivated as they each stared each other down before he turned in the opposite direction.*

Yeah, Mook drove a black Range Rover, rocked the hottest gear, wore high dollar jewelry and made it tsunami in the club, but there was nothing sexy about him at all. And he was still small time by Nessa's estimation. He was moving about two bricks a week, was still living in the projects and only had about two goons on his payroll. The shit definitely seemed like a little mom and pops operation to Nessa. It may have impressed the young teeny boppers around the 'hood who didn't know any better but it didn't faze Nessa in the least. She knew what real money and real power looked like.

Nessa was only twenty-one at the time, but had seen a lot and had experienced a lot. She remembered being a little girl and seeing her father's killers walking the project's roof tops with Choppers in their hands and ready to murder rival crews. She also recalled suitcases full of money, a fleet of cars, and goons that wouldn't allow anyone too close to him. She remembered it all. It was because of those memories that small timers like Mook couldn't impress her although she allowed them to think they could. Still though, despite her pretending, Nessa could never keep a muzzle over her mouth. She had a smart one, and that day, her disrespectful words made Mook snap on her.

Mook attempted to shit on another man that Nessa had simply waved to. When Mook told her not to speak to another male in his presence, Nessa belittled him by saying the guy had more money than him. And a bigger dick, too.

"Bitch, watch yo' mouth," he told her in front of

everyone.

"*Nigga, you small time,*" *she said.* "*I say what I want, when I want.*"

Before Nessa knew it, Mook backhanded her so hard she fell to the concrete. Standing over her, he yelled, "*I told you I'm tired of that mouth!*"

"*Fuck you!*" *she shouted back from the ground, before hock spitting on him, and commencing to talk more shit.* "*Wack ass nigga! Broke ass nigga!*"

"*What?*"

As the crowd gathered around, Nessa found it necessary to make him look like a fool in front of everyone. "*Little-ass dick having muthafucka!*"

Nessa's initial thought was to get to her purse so she could pull out the custom blade that was concealed in her lipstick tube. But Mook moved too fast. Mook swiftly and angrily dropped to his knees, pulled back his fist and prepared to hit her again. Before he could though, the man with the green eyes appeared. He looked like some type of business man; handsome, and with a bald head...a Michael Jordan clone just with slightly lighter skin and a set of perfectly white teeth. He didn't let the fact that he had on a pair of black Ferragamo loafers, black slacks, a crispy white button down keep him from getting his hands dirty.

Grabbing Mook, pulling him off of Nessa and tossing him on his ass, the man quickly got on top of Mook and yelled, "*Brother, that's a woman!*" *while punching him directly in the mouth.* "*You don't hit a woman. What the fuck is wrong with you?*"

He punched Mook again. This time the punch jerked Mook's head to the side so viciously that blood sprayed from his mouth. With no hesitation, the man snatched Mook up by the collar and hit him again with an even more brutal punch than before. Blotches and sprinkles of Mook's

82

blood were now on the man's white button down.

Nessa stared almost wide-eyed at the action. Mook's body was motionless. For a moment she thought he was possibly dead as each punch made his head jerk limply from side to side and blood poured from the side of his mouth onto the concrete beneath his skull.

Finally, the man climbed off of Mook's body, and headed over to Nessa. With blood on his hands, which didn't seem to faze him at all, he asked her, obviously and sincerely concerned, "You okay?"

Holding her jaw, she said, "Yeah."

"Let me see your jaw," he said smoothly.

She removed her hand.

Looking at it closely and not seeing any damage, he said, "Doesn't appear to be broken but you should still see a doctor just in case."

"I'm okay."

"My car is right over there," he said pointing across the street towards a glistening silver Jaguar F-type coupe parked at the curb. "I can take you to the hospital. It's really not a problem. Not a problem at all."

"I'll be fine," she assured him.

"I know you're fine. I just wanna make sure you're okay. Can I do that for you?"

His words warmed her heart. She nodded.

"What's your name?"

"Nessa."

"I'm Luke," he responded.

From then on, they were inseparable….modern day Bonnie & Clyde. Although Nessa had other intentions, she now couldn't shake him. Luke owned her mind, body and soul.

"Nessa, do you hear me?" Luke kept shouting through the phone.

Filthy Rich BY: KENDALL BANKS

Nessa finally snapped back to reality and began badgering him again. "Look-a-here, Luke, I need to know what your plans are? When are you coming back here?"

"I'm not sure. I'll let you know as soon as I know. For now go look in my closet. There's ten thousand in the Prada shoebox marked with a small X. That should hold you over for a few days."

"You think money is the answer to everything!" she shouted. "What about us? What about our plans for the future? You know I want to be married and start having kids in the next few years."

Silence filled the phone.

"You hear me, Luke?"

"I have no choice, Nessa."

"And what the fuck is that supposed to mean?"

Luke's line beeped. Nessa knew it was someone else calling into his line. Before she could fuss about that, Luke's next set of word's silenced her.

"This woman is calling again," he said suspiciously. "Some lady keeps calling my damn phone asking about you. She wants to know how she can get in touch with you. When I asked her how she knows you, she said it wasn't a good idea for me to know."

"Oh God," Nessa said in a low tone.

"Who the fuck is this lady? And how did she get my number, Nessa?" Luke questioned with a stern voice. "Did you give it to her? What's this about? You know how I feel about people having my number."

Suddenly, Nessa faked a stomach ache and rushed off the phone. The moment she hung up, her thoughts ran wild. "Oh, so she's ready for war?" Nessa chatted to herself.

****

84

Filthy Rich BY: KENDALL BANKS

Dressed in metallic Tory Burch flip-flops and an Alice & Olivia maxi dress, Nessa slid out of the driver's seat of Luke's Maserati, shut the door and made her way through the parking lot of the East Potomac Park. As she headed past benches, tables and joggers, she could see her father sitting at a bench at the far end of the walkway. The sight of him gave her an undesirable feeling in the gut of her stomach. She always got that feeling each time she laid eyes on him.

"Hey, baby," Byron Kingston happily greeted his daughter.

The two hugged. As they did, Nessa rolled her eyes. Her stomach grew slightly nauseous also at the smell of cheap liquor and cigarette smoke radiating from her father's body. God, how she hated the man he'd become.

Releasing his embrace, he admired his baby. "You look gorgeous as usual...looking like a bag of money." Developing a thoughtful expression, he told her, "You look just like your mother the day I met her. You're the spitting image."

Nessa gave no hint of being flattered. She recognized her father's intent. She knew the flattering compliment was simply his way of softening her up before he asked her for something. There was an ulterior motive. With him, there *always* was.

"Dad, look, what do you want?" she asked.

"To see you."

She didn't believe him for a second. She just wanted to get whatever he really wanted out of the way and leave. Just looking at him irked her last nerve.

Byron wasn't the man he used to be. Prison time, hard living and constant scheming had reduced him to a disappointing failure. Gone were the days of pretty Cadillacs, expensive clothes, blindingly bright jewelry, and pockets full of money. His clothes now looked as if they came from the Salvation Army. His transportation was the bus, which he rarely had money for. And his jewelry had been either sold or pawned.

"Dad, you said you needed to talk to me about something."

"Yeah, I did. But I wanted to see you, too. Can't a father want to see his child? Can't a father want to hug his daughter? I never get to see you."

"Cut the bullshit, dad! Don't try to guilt trip me to death. Don't try to sit here and act like you don't know why I don't come see you. You're always fucking scheming. You're always trying to get over on somebody. I don't have time for that shit."

"You're right, Nessa. I've made some mistakes."

"*Some?*"

"All right, a lot."

"Shit, even *a lot* is an understatement."

He dropped his head.

"For even a damn brief moment did you realize or even care that the decisions you were making and the life you were living would affect us? When you were killing people in front of me, did you ever stop to think that type of shit wasn't appropriate for a child to see?"

There was regret in his face and expression.

"Did you even care that I didn't even have my mother around to console me?"

"It's not my fault that she didn't want me or you."

"Nah, it was your fault. I know that now that I'm older."

"Nessa…I…"

"When the Feds kicked in our door and gave me to Children's Services, do you have any idea what I had to go through in those shelters and foster homes?"

Filthy Rich BY: KENDALL BANKS

Flashes of terrible traumatizing moments passed quickly through Nessa's mind, moments she was ashamed of, moments she had placed deeply into the farthest and darkest spaces of her memory. Her body could still feel the physical pain of the abuse. She could still hear her own screams, her own whimpers, her own pleading for mercy. Her nostrils could still remember the nauseating stench of a grown man's body. She could still remember being terrified each time her bedroom door would open at night.

"Nessa, I can't change the past."

"You're right. You sure can't."

"Besides, your mother was a hoe… that's why she got what she deserved."

Nessa threw her hands up and flicked him off. "Now what the hell did you call me for? What did you need to talk about?"

An uneasy look appeared on his face. Nessa knew exactly what the look meant. Pissed off, she said while shaking her head, "Once again, like a silly bitch I fell for it."

"Sweetheart…"

"How much?"

"Nessa, I..."

"How much!" she yelled.

A blank, devious expression appeared across his face.

Shaking her head once again, she went into her purse and counted two hundred dollars careful not let her father see exactly how much money she was actually carrying. "Here," she said, shoving the money towards him.

"Thanks, baby. I'm going to pay you back."

"Whatever."

What a poor excuse for a man he'd become, she thought to herself.

"Heard you got a new boyfriend," he told her while stuffing the money into the pockets of a pair of tight fitting pair of slacks that had gone out of style at least two decades ago.

Nessa's head turned like the demonic chick from the movie, *The Exorcist*. "How'd you hear that?"

"I've got ears."

His look had become more and more conniving.

"Look, I've gotta go."

"I want to meet him," he said sternly.

"People in hell want ice water. We can't all get what we want though. Besides, I told him your ass was dead."

Appearing hurt, he asked, "Why'd you do that?"

"Because in a lot of ways, you *are* dead to me."

Those words pierced Byron's heart. A cold expression began to fall over his face. With a serious tone, he said, "I may have done dirt, baby girl. But let's keep in mind that yo' track record ain't squeaky clean neither, ya hear?"

Nessa didn't reply. She knew exactly what her father was implying. If anything, she was surprised that he was bringing it up.

Seeing that his words had gotten to her, he said, "Yeah, you know what it is. Can't blame *that* particular moment on me, can ya?"

"You son of a bitch. You're actually bringing that up."

"Hell yeah, because you're trying to act like yo' shit don't stink. You got secrets too, Nessa. You made mistakes just like me. You got a secret. Now, how would you like it if I let yo lil' boyfriend in on that secret?"

She shook her head.

"Look, Nessa, I know about yo' situation. I know yo' man is loaded. I've heard all about him."

"And what does that have to do with you?"

"There's enough room on this gravy train for both of us. I don't want to step on yo' feet. Just let me get a few scraps."

Nessa had enough. "You know what, Dad. Go straight to fucking hell. Stay away from me and stay away from my man." She headed off.

Byron charged up on his daughter, snatched her around by the hand and then began to squeeze and twist it in a way that made Nessa feel like her wrist was going to snap. "Owwwwwww," she cried.

"Bitch, who the fuck do you think you're talking to?" he asked.

"You're hurting…"

"I'm yo' daddy, ho. I'm yo' family. And despite whether you like it or not, I'm still the only Goddamn family yo' ass got."

Nessa was nearly kneeling as her father applied the pressure to her hand and wrist. Tears were beginning to fall from her eyes; but not from fear. Nessa's emotional plight came from the fact that she was born to two fucked up people. She often wondered why she wasn't born to two loving, normal people. Ultimately, they made Nessa the woman she had become.

"Now, as I said, bitch, I want in. I want a nice piece of what you and this new nigga of yours got going on. If I don't get it, maybe we'll just have to see if he'll still love you after I expose yo' little secret."

Nessa was now crying profusely. The pain had become beyond unbearable.

"Choose wisely, Nessa. Choose yo' decision wisely, boo."

He let her hand go.

Holding her hand and wrist, Nessa hurriedly walked

off anxious to get away from her father.

With a smirk on his face, Byron shouted to her back, "I'll be in touch, baby girl with you *and* yo' boyfriend…You can count on it!"

Filthy Rich BY: KENDALL BANKS

Chapter 9

The towering Christian church on Decatur Street was breathtaking. Its tall and arched windows were painted with Biblical images along with its ceiling. Its floors were waxed. Its pews were polished and made of expensive imported wood. Porcelain statues of Jesus and Mother Mary were spread throughout. The darkness of the current moment left no interest in admiring the building's beauty or vast history.

From wall to wall, the church was packed with hundreds of people mourning Gavin's passing. Among them were Chetti, Darien and Luke. They sat in the front pew dressed in black. On the other side among friends and family sat Gavin's mother, Trinity. Amidst her broken heart, she was seething with hatred and fury. She rocked back and forth trying to hold it in as the Pastor stood speaking at the podium. Finally, unable to hold her tongue anymore, she stood and walked directly across the aisle to Luke, Darien and her mother, Chetti Bishop. Reaching them, she spit directly into Luke's face.

The Pastor stopped midsentence.

Gasps were heard.

Chatter began.

Of course some of the whispers referred to Trinity's bright red hair, multiple holes and earrings in her ear, and the nose ring dangling from her nose.

"You let my son die!" Trinity screamed at Luke. "You let 'em get killed!"

Keeping his composure, Luke accepted a handkerchief from Nessa and wiped the spit from his face.

"Baby, calm down," an elder from the church said as he tried to pull her back towards her seat.

"Get the fuck off of me!" Trinity yelled. "This is between me and my so called family! They let my son get murdered!"

"Control yo'self, bitch," Darien blurted as he stood from his seat.

"*Bitch?*" Trinity asked her brother in disbelief. "That's what I am to you these days?"

Luke stood from his seat and stood in between them. He felt even more awful knowing no one had told Trinity the truth. She had no idea that Luke had actually pulled the trigger. All she knew was that Gavin had been allowed to work with Luke and Darien against her wishes. Because of that she held them responsible.

"You muthafuckas murder my baby and have the nerve to call me a bitch?"

"You're making such a mockery of yourself," Chetti said to her daughter from underneath her fedora as she sat with her legs crossed. "Quit being so uncivilized." She shook her head. "Some folks are just so damn primitive."

"While you have the nerve to call *me* a bitch, *that's* the *bitch* right there!" Trinity pointed at her mother. "Look at her. Bitch sittin' there like she's Jackie Kennedy, like royalty, like butter wouldn't melt in her muthafuckin' mouth!"

Chetti sighed in annoyance, but arrogantly while shaking her head.

"Wasn't enough you had to lose your own son, huh?" Trinity asked her mother.

Those words cut Chetti. She glared at her daughter with spite.

"Yeah, I said it, bitch. It was you and this life that got my brother, Cedrick, killed!"

More chattering surrounded the feuding family.

"Or have y'all forgotten about him?"

As Nessa sat spectating, she was surprised to discover Luke had another brother. She'd never heard anything about him. There weren't even any pictures of him anywhere in the mansion. She'd prided herself on learning as much about the family as she could over the past year and a half; this news had her stumped.

Growing infuriated, Darien attempted to push his way by his brother. "Shut the fuck up Trinity before I slap yo' bitch ass to the floor!"

"Fuck you, Darien! I dare you to fuckin' touch me!" Trinity yelled back.

"Fuck *you*, bitch!"

Luke held his brother tightly.

Trinity turned her attention to her mother again. "Look at you sittin' there with that smug ass look on yo' face like you're better than everybody."

Smirking, Chetti said in the most stuck up way possible, "No, dear. Not everybody. But most definitely you."

Trinity charged at her mother. Several bystanders hopped up to grab her as Chetti made loud, degrading remarks. Trinity was pulled back before she could lay hands on her though.

"People don't know…this family's real fucked up!" Trinity belted to anyone listening then turned her attention back to her mother. "I hate you, you bitch!" she shouted. "You fucked up this family! It's all your fault!"

"Instead of hating me, you need to hate the booster who sold you that tacky ass outfit. And that ghetto ass hair…dear God," Chetti exclaimed with a strong, long exhale. "Now poof, be gone, bitch!"

More gasps and chattering. Even the Pastor began to say a prayer while the choir standing behind him stood in awe.

"I'm done keepin' your secrets, bitch!" Trinity yelled. "I'm done keepin' *all* of your secrets. I'm exposin' your asses right here and now!"

"Trinity, enough is enough," Luke told her.

"It ain't enough 'til I say it's enough!"

"Trinity…" Luke said again.

Snatching away from those who attempted to hold her back she headed toward the podium. Trinity shoved Pastor Grant to the side and grabbed the mic.

"What the hell is she doing?" Chetti asked no one in particular.

It was clear from the faces of Luke, Darien, and Chetti that Trinity had sparked fear in their souls. Whatever she was about to say had scared them all. The clearing of throats and gasps throughout the church became louder and louder. Darien's eyes shifted toward his mother and vice versa. They both looked toward Luke hoping he'd stop her.

"Ladies and gentlemen, I need to share some info with you," Trinity announced… "some old fashioned drama…soap opera type shit."

"Get here down from there!" Chetti shouted.

"Oh now you want me down, huh? Scared yo' lil' secret is about to get exposed?"

Chetti remained frozen.

Afraid.

Shocked.

"Do you all want to know who Gavin's father was?" Trinity asked the congregation.

All eyes were on her.

Goose bumps appeared on Chetti's entire upper body.

Darien froze.

Luke's body tensed.

Their reactions were all due to the fact that they knew who Gavin's father was.

"Gavin's father is..."

The entire space in the church had grown so quiet you could hear a pen drop.

Then...she said it.

"Luke Bishop, ladies and gentlemen. Yes, Luke Bishop, my own brother was the father of my child, my *dead* child!"

Eyes widened.

Disbelief registered on faces.

An older lady fainted.

Nessa looked at Luke with a twisted expression. *What in the fuck is going on,* she thought to herself.

"She's lying!" Chetti shouted, looking around at everyone in embarrassment. "She's a damn liar. She always has been. That's why we banished her from the family!"

"Men and women lie, mother. Blood tests don't! Now, tell the truth bitch!"

Chetti couldn't respond.

The church was now in chaos.

"And, bitch, you didn't banish me!" Trinity continued. "It was me who left y'all. I left because I didn't want my son to go through the fuckin' life you sent your own damn kids through. I didn't want him being forced to fuck his own sisters just to preserve the bloodline. "

Darien eyed his sister coldly.

Luke dropped his eyes to the floor.

"Yeah, the truth is out!" Trinity said. "Y'all ain't nothin' but a family of drug-dealin' incest-ass muthafuckas who kill people; all three of you!"

The Pastor dabbed a handkerchief across his forehead. He'd performed countless funerals but none like this one.

"I hope when you die, you all go directly to fuckin' hell. When you get there, I hope every single person you've killed is standing at the gate waitin' for your sick asses with a machine gun!"

Luke raised his eyes from the floor and looked at his sister.

Starring directly back into Luke's eyes, she said, "*Now* enough is enough."

With those words said, Trinity slammed the microphone to the ground and stormed out of the church. Unable to take the scrutiny, Chetti, Luke and Darien exited as well. Along with them were Nessa and Brandon. They each reached the entrance of the church, opened its doors and stepped out onto the steps.

Then…

Automatic gunfire rang out!

Bullets sprayed from two black Cadillac Escalades. Each ricocheted off the walls of the church. People began to scream. Amidst the chaos, Luke jumped on top of his mother and pulled her to the ground immediately. Strangely, she wasn't afraid. She squirmed for seconds trying to break free from Luke's protection.

"Get those muthafuckas!" Chetti shouted.

As the bodyguards scurried, Brandon remained on top of Nessa. The moment shots rang out he'd pulled her to the ground, covering her body in the form fitting Michael Costello dress.

"Muthafuckas!" Darien yelled furiously as he pulled a gun from inside his suit and began to return fire along with the family's security.

As the moment passed, the gunshots seemed to ring out forever although it was actually for several seconds. Finally, the shots ended and the Escalades sped off with the family's security darting down the church's steps continuing to spray shots.

"Ma, you okay?" Darien and Luke asked their mother as they helped her to her feet once the shots ceased.

"I'm alright," she told them. "It'll take a lot more than that shit to take me down," she bragged, wiping imaginary dust from her clothing.

"You okay?" Brandon asked Nessa as he helped her to her feet while inspecting her for blood.

"I'm good,' she told him.

"You sure?"

"Just shook up. But I'm okay."

The two looked at each other. The stare that they gave each other spoke volumes. It was just a step further from the look they gave each other back at the mansion the day Luke returned from being missing. There was now no doubt in Nessa's mind that she and Brandon were interested in each other.

"Those muthafuckas are going to pay!" Darien screamed. "They're goin' to fuckin' pay!"

Filthy Rich BY: KENDALL BANKS

Chapter 10

The dick shoved hard and deeply into Nessa with force. It made her thighs shiver, her adrenalin pump, her breathing accelerate, her toes curl. She moaned loudly as it continued its massacring destruction of her insides mixing her feelings with both pleasure and pain. She welcomed both.

Nessa looked up into the eyes of the man on top of her. So quickly, he'd taken a hold of her interests. So quickly he had become something she wanted, something she needed, no matter how bad the taboo.

From the look on Nessa's lover's face, he felt the same way she did. He'd wanted her from the moment he had first laid eyes on her. Now that he was inside her, *deeply* inside her, it felt amazing.

Although they'd been going at it for nearly an hour, it didn't take long for the fictional couple to switch positions. As he held her body bent over the chair, his plunges quickened.

"Mmmmmmmm," Nessa moaned. "Fuck me hard," her speech loud and slurred.

"This pussy is soooooo damn good," he hissed,

while slapping her on the ass.

Nessa, cooed like a baby then reached behind her scratching his thigh from top to bottom. She kept moving her hips back and forth so she could take in every inch of his shaft.

"Ohhh shit," he hollered as his thrust became more and more violent.

"Don't stop. Don't stop," Nessa shouted. "Right there. Oooooooooooh, damn, Brandon."

As his thrusts became faster and faster, Nessa wished it could last forever. Unfortunately though, it only lasted a few more seconds. Her pussy was too good. Her moans were too much of a turn on. He could no longer hold out.

Finally…

Despite how hard he fought to hold back…

Orgasm!

Both of their bodies intertwined with each other like snakes as they both exploded in unison. Their juices mixed together, neither of them wearing protection. They then lay together in each other's arms with their bodies convulsing and quivering for a moment.

"Damn, you got some good pussy!" Brandon shouted. "No wonder that nigga Luke moved you in his crib."

Nessa kept huffing and puffing without giving Brandon a response. She continued to feel light-headed and repeating her words over and over again, "What the fuck...what the fuck."

After several minutes of lying together, Nessa jumped as the reality dawned upon her. The room seemed to spin as her memory was beginning to fully come back. If their reality bothered Brandon he wasn't showing it. Nessa was the first to seem frazzled about what the two of them had just done. She was the first to develop a conscience.

I fucked Brandon? She thought to herself. *I fuckin' enjoyed it?*

The fact that they'd checked into the Ritz Carlton at Pentagon City intentionally proved that what they'd done was pre-meditated. Nessa placed her hands against her face and shouted. "This was so fuckin' wrong! Why did I...we...do this?"

Brandon had lifted himself onto one elbow. "Because I saved your life," he stated nonchalantly.

"Even though you saved my life earlier, this was such a mistake."

"Mistakes sometimes turn into positives," Brandon shot back.

"What kinda positive can come from this?" Her voice remained unusually loud as the alcohol kept her from controlling her tone.

Yes, Nessa had wanted to fuck Brandon even prior to the five lemon drops at a nearby bar, not far from the burial site. But she would've never gone through with it if she hadn't been so vulnerable and gotten overly intoxicated. Luke had instructed Brandon to watch over Nessa while only he, Darien and Chetti attended the burial. No one else, besides bodyguards, was allowed to come. Nessa expressed her disapproval. She wanted to be there for her man. But Luke didn't want to hear it. After the shootout, Luke just didn't feel the burial would be safe for Nessa. He didn't want to take a chance on her getting shot if the shooters decided to come back and finish what they started.

"You love Luke?" Brandon asked while reaching to grab Nessa's arm.

"Yep. More than I love myself."

"Even after what you heard today at the funeral?"
She paused for a moment.

"Hard to swallow, huh?" Brandon asked.

"Definitely. Did you know?"

"Nah, came just as much of a shock to me as it did
to you and everyone else. The Bishops have always been a
family shrouded in secrecy. Got to be that way though, in
the business they're in. The less people know about you,
the better."

"So, how does it feel to be a Fed and have a crooked
ass family?" Nessa asked.

Brandon seemed shocked as his eyebrows wrinkled.
"What are you talking about?"

"C'mon Brandon, I don't have time to sit here while
you play dumb. I know more than you think I do."

"Oh really?"

Nessa nodded. "Yes, Luke already told me everything."

Once again, Brandon seemed surprised. He moved
away from Nessa and sat up completely. He eyed her in-
tently.

"He already tested my loyalty though, so don't
worry about me going around town telling people your secret and shit," Nessa informed as she thought back to the
torment that night.

"Well, if you know so much, why are you drilling
me?"

"I want to know more. I want to make sure I'm not
putting myself in jeopardy. I already know about the millions in the cash room in the basement. I know about
Luke's stash houses. I know about the twenty million in
offshore accounts…"

She paused after seeing the surprise in Brandon's
eyes.

"…And I even know Luke's coke supplier, Chavez. I met him once about a month ago." She paused again.

"So, what else do I need to know?"

"Look, you've said enough as far as I'm concerned."

"Brandon, I could've been killed today. Those bullets just missed my ass. I deserve to know *something*."

"Look, all I can tell you is that the Bishops are at war with an enemy that has no problem killing to get what it wants."

"I know who that enemy is."

He looked at her strangely. "What?"

"I heard you guys talking in the den the boardroom when Chetti threw me shade."

"You did, huh?"

She nodded.

"What'd you hear?"

"Everything."

He sighed. "Darien had pissed those guys off. That's why they had the balls to come shoot up the funeral. He's been making moves against them without family permission or knowledge. That's all I'm saying."

She grew silent, thinking for a moment.

Brandon looked at her seriously. "Nessa, the Bishops aren't anything to play with. They're lethal. They're more dangerous than anyone in your scariest dreams. That includes Luke as well. Don't get it twisted. For your own good, don't go listening to conversations you're not supposed to be a part of. Their secrets are secrets worth murdering for. Trust me on that one. They will kill you if they even *think* you know something you shouldn't."

She curled up into a ball with shivers running down her spine. She thought about the many times she'd crept around the house searching for information.

"You didn't answer *my* question," he said.

"Which one?"

"Do you still love him after what you discovered about him today?"

She paused at the question just like she had before. What she'd discovered about Luke and Trinity sharing a child today really did bother her. It was disappointing and disgusting, but was more confusing than anything. Also, she was feeling some kind of way about how when the bullets began flying, he didn't seem to care about her wellbeing. He dove on top of his mother immediately while never bothering to look Nessa's way. Even when the bullets stopped flying, he didn't even bother to ask Nessa if she was okay. He simply gave orders to Brandon and shoved Nessa in a limo without so much as a kiss or an "I love you". Still though, answering Brandon's question, she said, "Yeah, I love him."

He stared at her for a moment then leaned in, kissing her on the forehead. "So does that mean what we've done is just a one-time thing?"

Nessa didn't answer immediately. She had to think about the best way to answer the question. After all, Brandon did have some very good dick and would be a great ally for what she had planned...but she loved Luke. The thought of betraying him sickened her.

"I really want to see you again," he told her.

"That means I'll be planning to cheat. I consider what I did a mistake."

Brandon laughed. "Yeah, my dick accidentally fell into your pussy." His tone became more serious as he added, "No, seriously, I really do want to see you again."

She thought hard about how great he'd fucked her. "I'll think about it. I care about Luke and will someday be his wife."

At that moment, Brandon stood up completely naked, allowing Nessa to examine his nine inch, soft dick.

"Wishful thinking, but okay. I'ma be president one day, too." He shook his head. "I gotta go take a shower."

"Don't be an asshole," Nessa mumbled as he walked off.

Nessa lay there alone thinking about what she'd just done. She wished she hadn't gone to that bar with Brandon. She wished she had never taken the first drink, and definitely not the ones that followed. Then Luke's face entered her mind and remained there. She knew she was betraying him but decisions had to be made. She honestly felt bad, but riding both sides of the fence wouldn't fly much longer.

Moments passed.

Nessa grabbed her phone from her purse. Looking at the screen, she saw that her father had called twice. She also had a few missed calls from Sidra. She wasn't eager to return any of them at the moment. She then noticed a missed text. Pulling it up, she discovered it was from Chetti. Immediately, she thought how odd that was since Chetti never called or texted her. Nessa read the message.

My eyes may be ageing along with everything else on my body but despite their age, they see EVERYTHING...

Including what your sneaky ass is doing right NOW.

Chills immediately ran down Nessa's spine so badly that her hands trembled and she dropped the phone. Was Chetti really watching her right now, she wondered.

Chapter 11

Luke, Darien and Chetti all sat at the table in the den when Trinity was brought in kicking, punching and scratching. The two bodyguards worked extra hard to keep her arms controlled. Obviously pissed off, she screamed, "Get the fuck off me. Put me down!"

"Don't bring that hoodrat shit into my home, Trinity!" Chetti shouted.

Approaching the far end of the table, the bodyguards released Trinity. Immediately she turned to them and spit in their faces. Controlling their composure, they simply closed the door, placed their backs to it and faced the room while wiping off their faces.

Seething, Trinity turned to her estranged family and stared daggers through them. Her hatred for each of them was written all over her face. "So, what did you bring me here for?" she asked. "To kill me, huh? Is that it?"

No one said anything.

Trinity spread her arms. "Alright, here the fuck I am. What are you waiting for? Do the shit then!"

"Such a fucking drama queen," Chetti stated, shaking her head while sipping a glass of tequila. "She always was. I see nothing's changed."

"Fuck you!" Trinity screamed across the room at her.

Chetti chuckled. She loved the way she always got up underneath her daughter's skin without having to try hard.

"Kill me, muthafuckas! Let's get the shit over with!" Trinity yelled out.

Darien didn't say anything. He just sat silently. The expression on his face though clearly expressed he hadn't forgiven her for spilling personal family business at the funeral the day before. He still wanted to slap the taste out of her damn mouth for that stunt. However, for the moment Darien decided to keep his feelings to himself.

"No one's going to kill you," Luke told his sister. "No one's going to touch you."

"And I'm supposed to believe you?" Trinity questioned.

"You've got my word," Luke responded.

Trinity calmed slightly at those words. Luke had always been a man of his word. But her mother and Darien were snakes. They would look Jesus himself in the face with a smile and a lie then stab him in the back as soon as his back was turned. Those two could never be trusted. Luke though, wasn't cut that way. His word along with loyalty meant something sacred to him. He never gave neither unless he meant to do right by them.

"Have a seat," Luke told his sister.

"No, I prefer to stand," Trinity replied.

"Well, let the dumb bitch stand until her legs are sore," Chetti said. "And that horrible red hair," she added. "Who gets their hair shaved on one side? Despicable!"

"You miserable bitch!" Trinity spewed.

"That's *Mrs*. Miserable Bitch to you. No problem

though. No harm done. I understand the mistake. Welfare bitches like yourself don't quite know how to recognize women of my caliber." She smirked before continuing, "And somebody pleaseeeeeeee snatch that nose ring from her nostril. It's appalling."

"Ladies," Luke interjected. "Will you *please* cease the insults for a moment?"

The ladies silenced but that didn't stop them from staring at each other like two professional boxers on fight night.

"Trinity, you're here because of what happened yesterday," Luke told his sister. "You're here because of the attack on our family."

"The shooting has nothing to do with me."

"Not directly of course. But the killers' intentions were made very clear. They will kill whoever they must to destroy this family," Luke informed.

"Look, Luke, whatever y'all got yourselves into, that's on y'all. That's your fucking business. Leave me the hell out of it," Trinity replied.

"I'm afraid that's not possible. You know we would never purposely involve you in harm's way, Trinity. But the situation we're involved in currently can't be taken lightly. The men who shot up the funeral yesterday will kill whoever they need to, including you, just to get to us."

"Hell no. I'm not staying here with a bunch of fucking liars and crooks," Trinity stated firmly, while crossing her arms. "I would trust a stranger off the damn street before I trust any of y'all ever again!"

"Fuck this… just let her leave then, Luke. I'm sick of her mouth," Chetti said.

Trinity looked at her mother with disgust. "After everything you've put me through, I don't give a fuck what you're sick of. Fuck you and this so called *family*." Trinity then looked at her two bothers. "All I want from either one of you is to find Gavin's killer. I won't sleep until the muthafucka who pulled the trigga is 6 feet under! Do y'all have any leads yet?"

"No, but we're still looking," Luke uttered, unable to look Trinity in the face. "See, we all have the same goal in mind."

"But I'm still not staying here," she shot back.

"Well, fuck it," Darien said, losing his patience. "If the bitch don't want to be here, let her ass stay out there bobbin' and weavin' bullets like Floyd Mayweather if she wants to."

"I second that motion," Chetti said.

"Fuck all of you!" Trinity turned and headed for the door. "I'm leaving!"

The two bodyguards placed themselves shoulder to shoulder blocking Trinity's way.

"I'm afraid that's not possible, Trinity," Luke told her.

Turning around, she said, "Luke, let me out of here."

"In due time. I promise you that. But until we get this current situation handled, the family compound is your new home. It's the safest place for you right now."

"Luke, this is fuckin' kidnapping. You can't keep me here against my fuckin' will!"

"I'm displeased that you see it that way, Trinity. But I assure you it is necessary."

Chetti shook her head. "Reminds me of a dog trapped in a bear trap growling and biting at the people trying to free him. The dumb bitch can't even recognize when someone's trying to save her life. Where the hell were you when God passed out brains?"

"I don't know," Trinity snapped back. "Probably the

same place your ass was when he was passing out a con-science, you cold blooded bitch."

The two women once again glared at each other like cats.

"Trinity, your room is still the same," Luke said. "It hasn't been touched since you moved out."

The expression on Trinity's face clearly showed she didn't want to stay.

"Sis, please understand that my intentions aren't to make you miserable. They're just to keep you safe. No matter what our problems or beefs with each other, I my-self refuse to leave you among the wolves. You're still family."

In her heart, those words really did mean something to Trinity mainly because she knew Luke meant them. Sighing, she said, "Alright but as soon as this shit is over, I want out."

"No problem."

"I mean it, Luke."

"Trust him, Trinity," Darien said. "No one wants yo' ungrateful ass here no longer than you need to be. Shit, if it was up to me, yo' ass would be out there fending for yo'self."

Getting fed up with the unnecessary snaps, Luke slammed a fist down on the table. "Damn it, Darien!" he roared. "That's enough. Trinity is our baby sister. Like it or not, she's our flesh and blood. So from here on out, she will be treated with respect!"

Darien didn't respond. Luke being ten years older had always carried weight so he let his brother's words reign.

Luke nodded to the bodyguards blocking the door. They parted and opened the door for Trinity. Giving her brothers and her mother one final look, she left the room.

The room stood silent for several moments.

"Mom, I'm moving out in twelve days, the moment my place is ready," Luke finally said.

"What do you mean?" she asked.

"I already told you that I was walking away from the family business."

"But we're in the middle of a war."

"And I'm going to help see us through this war. I'm still moving though."

Darien shook his head.

"What are you shaking your head for?"

"What happened to loyalty?" Darien questioned.

"Loyalty, huh?"

"Yeah, nigga, loyalty. Did you forget what the fuck that is?"

"This coming from the same man who hadn't informed the rest of the family that he's been giving the go-ahead on attacks and drive-bys without the family's permission."

"What?" Chetti asked. "What are you talking about? You can't be fucking serious!"

Brandon had already told Luke about Darien's moves.

"That's why they shot up the funeral, Mother," Luke said.

Chetti looked at Darien like he was crazy. "You son of a bitch!" she screamed.

Darien developed an expression on his face like he'd just been filled with the fear of God. No human being on earth brought that expression out of him except his mother. Holding his hands in front of him defensively, he said, "Now, Ma, don't over react."

Before he could finish talking, his mother's drink filled his entire face.

With the liquid dripping down his lips he spoke slowly. "Mother, I just felt it was best we…"

"Nigga, you don't decide what's best for this family!" Chetti screamed at her son after slapping him harshly. The sound was loud and piercing.

Smirking at his brother, Luke stood from the table and headed towards the door. Walking out of the room and shutting the door amidst Chetti's cursing and yelling, he left his brother to suffer their mother's wrath.

In Luke's bedroom, Nessa sat in a chair staring into the vanity mirror while doing her makeup and combing her hair. Nervously, she thought about the threatening messages she'd gotten earlier on her phone. She thought about her devious father, and how she'd definitely get rid of him. It was certain, he had to go. She even thought about more ways to seek revenge on Luke's mother. Hundreds of thoughts seemed to whip through her mind, but most of her thoughts related to Brandon.

Nessa hadn't slept with another man since meeting Luke. She loved everything about him; the way he talked, walked, and carried himself. She especially loved the way he took care of her, leaving her wanting for nothing. She knew how Luke felt about loyalty but sex with Brandon had done something to her. It was different, exciting, rough, thuggish, all the things Luke had been missing lately.

Nessa looked down at her phone and sent a message to Sidra. She needed someone to bounce her thoughts off of.

What do you think Luke would do if I ever decided to cheat, Nessa texted.

Bitch, who did you fuck, Sidra replied.

Nobody. I'm just saying?

Loose booty, you think I'm stupid? Call me right now.

I can't

Why not?

'Cause I'm busy.

A'ight hoe. Call me when you get off the dick.

Although not in the laughing mood, Nessa couldn't help but to chuckle. Her friend was crazy. She kept brushing her hair until a voice sounded.

"So, you're the apple of my brother's eye these days?" Trinity said to her from the doorway.

Nessa turned. For a moment she didn't quite know how to react or what to say. After what she'd discovered at the funeral, the moment between she and Trinity seemed awkward to her.

Walking across the bedroom and extending her hand, Trinity introduced herself. Accepting her hand, Nessa smiled and introduced herself also. It seemed weird shaking the hand of a woman who resembled Chetti Bishop, Nessa's arch enemy in so many ways. All of the Bishops had high cheek bones, smooth, rich looking skin, and narrow, noses. It seemed to be a family trademark with the exception of Luke.

"My brother has good taste," Trinity said genuinely. "You're very beautiful."

Nessa smiled graciously. "Thank you."

"How long have you guys been together?"

"Almost two years."

"Uh-oh, must be something special in you for him to stick around that long."

"I hope."

"Trust me, sweetheart; there is. I know my brother.

115

He wouldn't go through trouble of being with you for this amount of time and moving you into the family home if he didn't think you were worth it. 'Cause Lord knows both my brothers are hoes; especially Darien. I'm expecting the nigga's dick to fall off any day now."

They both laughed.

Those words meant the world to Nessa.

"How are you getting along with my mother?"

"She's pretty cool," Nessa lied.

With an expression on her face that clearly showed she wasn't buying it, Trinity said, "Pretty cool, huh?"

Nessa didn't want to say anything more out of respect for Trinity.

Trinity smiled. "Sweetheart, it's okay. You can say it."

"Okay, she's a little rough around the edges."

"Rough around the edges? Girl, please. She's a pure, unadulterated, full-blooded bitch."

Nessa giggled.

Trinity smacked her lips. "Girl, it is what it is. She's a bitch to everybody, not just you. There's no way around that shit."

Nessa laughed again.

Trinity seemed to lighten up even more, marching around the room with her head held high, imitating her mother.

Nessa liked Trinity right then and there. She seemed down to earth and easy to get along with.

Both women laughed even more as Trinity mocked her mother's outrageous sayings and antics.

"Trinity," a man's voice suddenly spoke.

The laughter ended and both women looked to the doorway to see Luke standing there with a stone expression on his face. Sighing, Trinity told Nessa, "Nice to meet you, Sweetie. We'll see each other around."

"Nice to meet you, too."

Trinity left the bedroom but not before cutting her eyes at Luke as she rudely brushed by him.

"I like your sister," Nessa said. "She's real cool."

Approaching Nessa, he said, "Don't grow too attached. The two of you won't be together for too long."

"What's that supposed to mean?"

Luke's facial expressions had Nessa on edge. He seemed different; like something was bothering him.

"Nessa, you're starting to ask too many questions. My mother and Trinity just don't get along, that's all. Besides, my mother doesn't even think you're good for me, so chill."

Nessa didn't push the issue. If anything, she was still on edge about Chetti's text the day before. She wasn't quite sure if Chetti really did know she and Brandon were fucking or if she was simply trying to scare her. If she did though, Luke hadn't mentioned it, at least not yet.

She got up from the chair, and walked over to wrap her arms around her man. "I miss you, Luke. We haven't spent any time together lately."

Quickly, he removed her hands and stepped away.

"We're moving out of here in about two weeks," Luke said. "For now, I'll stay in a hotel to keep the peace with my mother."

"Well, I'm going with you."

"No, not a good idea. You'll be safer here for now," he stated firmly.

She smacked her lips and gave up the puppy dog face. "This is bullshit, Luke. And where in the hell are we moving?"

"It's a surprise."

"Well, can I furnish the home?"

"Whatever your heart desires."

Silence.

The elephant in the room couldn't be ignored any longer.

"Was Trinity's son really your child?" Nessa asked.

"I don't wish to discuss that."

"But."

"Nessa, there are some things about my life that you are just much better off not knowing. The less you know about me and this family, the better off you will be."

Nessa didn't quite like that answer but she had no choice but to accept it.

"Now, I've got to go handle some business," he told her after kissing her on the cheek. "Here's three grand. Start picking us up some necessities; sheets, towels, dishes and whatever else you think we'll need."

Nessa's disapproval showed on her face but she didn't say anything about the move. She desperately needed them to remain in the mansion. She did however feel it was a great time to ask about his plans with her.

"Are you ever going to propose, Luke?"

"Ahhh, c'mon, Nessa. Not now. I can't with the sympathetic shit. There's a time and place for everything," he told her firmly as he jetted to the door.

"When will you be back?" she yelled toward Luke's back." 'Cause we *are* going to discuss this. I'm not shacking up forever," she warned.

"Not sure." He ended with a shrug. "I'll be in touch."

Nessa stood looking stupid until Luke turned to ask, "You sure there's nothing you want to tell me?"

She shook her head profusely. Luke could've been asking for many reasons. But Nessa had learned from the streets to never shoot yourself in the foot. She'd no doubt take her secrets to her grave.

She hated to let him go but it was what it was. As he disappeared from the room, she headed to the window and stared down at the circular driveway waiting for him to exit the house. Moments later, flanked by bodyguards, she watched as Luke stepped into the night air, and slid into the back of a SUV. Seconds later, followed by two tinted out bulletproof SUVs filled with gunmen, he left the compound.

Alone again and bored, Nessa walked out of the bedroom not sure where to go or what to do. The heels of her Stilettos clicked loudly along the floor's surface and echoed throughout the hollow walls. She made her way through hallway after hallway with no destination in mind. Eventually, not by design, she found herself outside the door that had drawn her curiosity many times before.

"It's just a room where my mother keeps old things," Luke's words repeated themselves in Nessa's head.

There was something about the room that just didn't sit well with Nessa. Something about it gave her the creeps. She knew there was something behind its door much more than just a few "Old Things."

Now stepping closer to the door, Nessa placed an ear to the door and listened for several moments. She heard nothing. She then attempted to turn the knob. It was locked though. Backing away, she heard something shuffling around inside the room. Quickly, she once again placed an ear to the door.

Silence.

"Hello," she called.

No answer.

"Is anyone in there?"

Still no answer.

"Hello?"

Still silence.

Then…

BOOM!!!!!

Something crashed loudly against the other side of the door so hard, it startled Nessa enough to make her stumble backwards almost tripping over her feet. Now scared, she darted off down the hallway while repeatedly looking back at the door. But although scared, she was now absolutely convinced *someone* not *something* was in that room.

Filthy Rich BY: KENDALL BANKS

Chapter 12

"Fucking ungrateful sons of bitches," Chetti muttered angrily, speaking of all her children as she turned the locks on the door of Cedrick's room and make-shift prison cell. She walked boldly inside with her shoulders holstered and tightened fist to her sides. Two of the family's henchmen accompanied her.

As usual, Cedrick sat still in his chair while staring out his barred window, on the west wing, an unoccupied side of the house. His brain was mush, illogical thoughts and realities going through his head. Like always, he stunk of urine.

With a thick leather belt in her hand, Chetti began to pace the bedroom with rage in her eyes. "Fuckin' ungrateful bastards and bitches."

Cedrick didn't look at his mother. To him, no matter how mad she was or how much she paced, it was like she wasn't there. The medication simply gave him the power to tune her out.

"*This* is the shit that your great grandfather was trying to avoid when he decided to include incest in the origins of this dynasty," Chetti said to Cedrick while not looking at him but continuing to pace back and forth. "This is the shit right here."

Cedrick continued to show no signs of hearing her or caring about what was bugging her.

"He wanted the bloodline to remain strong and pure. He wanted us to breed with each other just like thorough-breds. Sure, I was against it when I first heard of it, but your father and his father were geniuses. They wanted to raise a family and dynasty of hustlers, a family and dynasty of street smart businessmen and women."

The two henchmen stood by looking and gawking. Chetti eyed them as she continued.

"That strategy made the Bishop's strong. It made us powerful. It made us Gods and goddesses among mortals. It made us who the fuck we are…

"Special." She paused before flipping out on her henchman. "And what the fuck are you all staring at! Stay the fuck out of Bishop business! Do you muthafuckers hear me?"

Quickly, they both turned and faced the wall.

Rage began to build in Chetti as she focused back to Cedrick. "But what the fuck do my ungrateful ass children want to do with what the fuck we've built, huh? What do they want to do? They want to piss it all away!"

Chetti snatched a lamp from the nightstand and slammed it against the wall so hard it shattered. Thousands of tiny shards of porcelain fell to the floor.

Cedrick still remained silent. He remained in his own world. Nothing or no one existed to him right now.

"My fuckin' son, Luke wants to take the family cor-porate!" she screamed. "He wants to leave this life, the life that made him a multimillionaire. He wants to question my power and my decision making like I haven't maneuvered this damn family to victory after victory after the death of your father!"

She kicked over a table.

"He even has the audacity to bring a *whore* into this family. He's flaunting the bitch in front of me, fucking her in my damn house, falling in love with that tramp!"

She was furious.

"I swear on my life that if he makes a baby with that worthless tramp, I'll kill it before I let it wear the name Bishop. I'll kill it dead. I'll personally bash that little fucker's head in with a ball ping hammer. I swear to God I will!"

She paced more relentlessly than before.

"And Darien, the hardheaded bastard. He's out here making moves without my Goddamn permission. He's out here going to war without me pressing the button!"

Cedrick continued to ignore his mother. Even if he was paying attention, her problems were her own, not his.

"I'm the fuckin' king and queen of this dynasty. *Me* Goddamn it. Me!"

Seconds passed.

"And Trinity." The name rolled off Chetti's tongue like horse manure. The expression on her face twisted. "The bitch spilling family business at the damn funeral like there aren't consequences. The bitch thinks I'm going to let that slide. She thinks shit's sweet. Well, I swear here and now she's got another muthafuckin' thing coming. No one crosses this family and gets away with it. No one, not even family members, are above ramifications and repercussions. That funky bitch is going to be handed consequences. I promise."

Chetti headed to the window, blocking Cedrick's view. With her back to him, she remained silent for several moments, still holding the belt. Finally, she turned to him. "And *you*," she said speaking to Cedrick. "Look at you.

Just a sorry, meaningless piece of blood and flesh not worth the piece of paper your birth certificate was made of. I should've aborted your sorry ass."

Cedrick didn't respond.

"To think your damn father had such high hopes for you."

Cedrick's expression remained the same. His demeanor remained the same.

Taking a step closer to her son and shaking her head, she said, "Sorry bastard can't even eat my damn pussy right. How the fuck could your weak ass be a proper general?"

She looked at her son like he was the scum of the earth. Then, with no warning, she raised the belt and…

SMACK!!!!!

The sound of the belt connecting with Cedrick's face gave off a sound so loud it echoed.

"All of you bastards and bitches had better realize I'm the head of this family!"

SMACK!!!!!

The belt swatted Cedrick's arm causing him to jump up and dash.

"Don't you run from me!"

Chetti gave chase and swung the belt wildly at her son's burly back. Each time it connected, he let off a yelp or scream.

"Ughh!!" he grunted.

As more lashes connected his shouts and screams became louder. "Ugh, Ugh! "

"Stop running!" Chetti shouted.

Suddenly, Cedrick tripped and fell.

Furious at all her children, she towered over her son and began to take all her frustrations out on him. Every swing was an attempt to beat his limbs off. As he curled into a fetal position to protect himself from the lashes, Chetti beat every vulnerable part of his body she could, including his face. She made sure that his shirt lifted so that lashes could connect with his back.

"Take it, you weak son of a bitch!"

Cedrick yelled. He screamed even more.

"Take it muthafucka. Take it! I'm the head fuckin honcho around here."

The belt rained down on Cedrick repeatedly. To his surprise, Chetti's goons never turned round. There was no hope for him as several gashes on his skin began to sting horribly.

Then finally…

Surprising to Chetti…

Cedrick reached out and caught the belt in the palm of his hand while in mid-swing. He then gave her a glare that she'd never seen come from his eyes before, a glare that expressed a yearning for revenge.

The room fell silent.

No words were spoken.

No movements at all.

The two henchmen turned around, and upon seeing Cedrick with one end of the belt clutched in the palm of his hand, they stepped forward.

Swiftly, Cedrick stood while continuing to glare directly into his mother's eyes. His six foot four muscular physique standing before her spoke volumes. Chetti's body tensed for a moment. She was caught off guard.

Cedrick stood face to face with his mother; his stance like that of a Mandingo warrior.

He didn't move.

He simply stared and remained frozen as blood dripped from different parts of his body.

The two henchmen began to make their way across

the room to assist their boss lady.

"Stay where you are," Chetti scolded without looking at them.

They froze.

Although surprised, refusing to show fear, Chetti looked Cedrick in the face and asked, "You got balls now, you little bitch?"

He didn't answer. His glare remained though.

"Do you?"

He stayed silent.

"You want to do something? You want to jump, bitch?"

He just eyed her.

"I didn't think so. Now let the belt go."

He continued to hold it, tightly.

"I said let it go, damn it!"

Moments passed.

The henchmen were on standby.

Then…

Cedrick finally did as he was told.

Smirking, Chetti stepped so close to her son, their lips were nearly touching. Looking him directly in the eyes, she said, "You may be a thirty-five year old man, but if you *ever* look at me like that again, I'll kill your worthless ass."

Then…

SMACK!!!!!

She swatted him across the face once more with the belt. She then walked off leaving him to hold his face, two thick welts showing across it clearly. Reaching the door, she said, "Oh, almost forgot."

Cedrick looked at her from across the room.

Pulling out two pills, she tossed them on the floor and said, "Eat up, Bitch! And since you showed some balls, I won't give you the needle tonight." She then walked out the room along with her bodyguards and locked the door.

Cedrick walked across the room and picked up the pills. He wanted so badly to take them. Like always, they were calling his name. Like always, he needed them to help him through this living hell.

He knew how sadistic his mother was. He knew she'd stolen his life and dreams but she'd gotten out of hand with her cruelty. Something had to change. Something had to be done. His mental state was now playing tricks on him. The pills in his huge hands were calling him. As he looked down at them he thought about the things his father shared with him before his death. There were so many things no one knew but him. He had to escape the life Chetti had built for him in between those four walls. It was time to expose everything.

The urge to swallow the pills continued.

The need for revenge filled him.

Up until now the last four years of his life had been a repeat; torture, pills, and sex with his mother. Cedrick knew taking the meds would ease the pain.

For some reason though, this time he decided to ignore his urge. Instead of taking them, he headed to the bathroom and did something he'd never done before...

He flushed them.

Dear Diary

The plot thickens. I keep giving this bitch more chances. But she keeps testing me. I want what's rightfully mine. And I will get it. No nigga who comes against me will live. Things about to change. Meanwhile…this nigga can fuck!

Chapter 13

"Did you get what I sent, Baby Girl?" Byron asked his daughter through the phone.

"Don't call me that," Nessa told him. "Don't ever call me that. I'm not your damn baby girl."

"Whatever."

Lying beside the pool in a sexy gold embroidered two-piece bathing suit, she asked, "And what are you talking about? What do you mean?"

"Did you get what I sent to the mansion?"

Growing nervous, Nessa arose from the plush chaise and asked, "How the fuck do you know this address?"

Chuckling, he answered, "Don't worry about that. All you need to know is I'm not playing with yo' ass. This process needs to be sped the fuck up. And the little video I sent should be yo' damn incentive to make that happen."

Nessa grew far beyond nervous. "What video?" She stood up and began pacing.

He chuckled once again. "I think you know the answer to that."

Flashes of violence appeared in Nessa's mind,

flashes of a moment long ago, a moment she'd regretted the very second it happened. Thoughts scrambled through her head. Then noises came from behind.

Sliding a glass door open, Trinity walked outside, carrying a bucket of ice with two champagne bottles inside. "What's up?"

Seeing Trinity, Nessa lowered her voice and whispered angrily, "Dad, don't send anything else to this damn house. Do you hear me?"

"You're not in the position to give orders, bitch. Now as I said, that video better be enough to make you get yo' damn priorities straight. If it ain't, I'll get even more ugly."

"You sneaky bastard, you…"

The line went dead before Nessa could finish her sentence.

"What's good, Nessa?" Trinity asked when she walked up in a super revealing two piece bathing suit that showed off her entire hour glass shape. She took a seat in a nearby chair.

Still feeling chills run down her spine from the phone call, Nessa said, "Just relaxing." Quickly, she sat back down trying to gather her thoughts.

Trinity kicked off her flip flops and lay back on her lounger underneath the sunshine. "I've got to admit this is about the only thing I missed about this house."

"How long has it been since you've been gone?" Nessa asked trying to get her father out of her mind.

"Long enough."

"Wowwwww, was it easy to leave all this behind?"

"Sweetheart, let me school you on somethin' real quick. Money, cars and mansions are nice. There's no doubt. But that shit don't compare to a piece of mind. That shit don't compare to bein' able to get up every mornin' and look yo'self in the eyes through the mirror with a clear conscience. Wealth can't buy that."

Nessa couldn't see walking away. Shit, life couldn't get any better than this.

"Don't get me wrong though," Trinity continued. "I didn't leave broke. I had a million in the bank and the family, specifically Luke, kicks me down a nice piece of change each month so I don't really want for shit."

Hate immediately rolled through Nessa's veins when she thought about Luke sending Trinity child support money. She was the one who wanted to be getting support from Luke. The *only* one.

"Were you involved in the family business?" Nessa finally asked.

Trinity looked at Nessa. Fire imaginarily exploded from her nose.

"I'm sorry," Nessa said quickly. "That was too personal."

"No, it's cool. I don't have a problem answering the question," Trinity said. "Yeah, I dabbled. I ran some guns, sold some drugs, and squeezed some triggers. Shit, I'm still a wild bitch at times. It runs in the blood. I still ride motorcycles, smoke weed and go to the shooting range. This family instilled that shit in me. I can't let it go. But for the sake of my son; God, bless the dead, I left the extreme parts of the family business alone. My baby needed a mother, not a loose bitch."

The two grew silent.

"So, since you didn't have nice things to say about your mother when I first met you and you basically called her a bitch, I guess you all don't get along, huh?" Nessa asked.

"I hate her ass actually," Trinity confirmed. "That's one evil bitch. She's done some foul shit that I will never fuckin' forgive her for."

"If you don't mind me asking, how long has the incest been going on?" Nessa finally asked.

Rising from her seat and swinging her feet over the side, Trinity gave Nessa a stern look. "Nessa, I like you, and evidently my brother *loves* you. You seem like cool peoples. But don't get it twisted."

Nessa figured she'd rubbed Trinity the wrong way.

"Never feel that shit's sweet enough for you to ask questions like that," Trinity continued. "These walls have ears; every last one of them. They hear everything. And askin' questions like that can get you killed."

Nessa didn't quite know how to respond; especially after seeing Trinity look around. She then stood up and grabbed a bottle of Champagne from the bucket.

"Even Luke won't be able to help you. Shit, it'll possibly be him who'll give the damn order to have you murdered and have yo' body thrown in a fuckin' incinerator somewhere."

Trinity popped the cork of her favorite champagne, Veuve Clicquot and poured herself and Nessa a glass before sitting back down.

Before Nessa could give what she'd said serious thought, her cell alerted her of an incoming text. Grabbing the cell from a glass table beside her, Nessa pulled up the text. She had several.

I WANT SOME MORE OF THAT PUSSY, the text read. It was from Brandon.

DON'T COME AT ME LIKE THAT, Nessa returned.

I WANT SOME TONIGHT.
YOU KNOW I CAN'T.
YOU CAN AND YOU WILL. MEET ME AT THE HOTEL TONIGHT AT EIGHT O'CLOCK!!!!!

Filthy Rich BY: KENDALL BANKS

AND IF I DON'T?

LET'S JUST SAY YOU DON'T WANNA GET ON MY BAD SIDE, NESSA. SEE YOU TONIGHT.

Nessa knew she'd created a monster.

Another text came through. This time though, it was Luke. He began asking her how she was doing. Instead of texting back, she called.

"Hey, Luke baby," she greeted him when he answered. She stood from the chaise and began to walk along the side of the pool. Her emotions were now running high. Nessa had been feeling really anxious and unsure about how things were playing out in her life.

"You okay?" he asked.

"I'm good. I miss you."

"As you should."

"Can't wait until we move in together."

"Looking forward to it myself."

"But are you sure we should do it now? Are you sure we shouldn't wait?"

The previous day, Luke had taken Nessa by the condo he was planning on moving her into. It was in a nice quiet Bethesda neighborhood, but it wasn't a mini- mansion or anywhere near as spectacular as the family compound. When Nessa asked why such a drastic difference, Luke told her he didn't want flashiness anymore. Flashiness brought attention from the wrong people. Nessa on the other hand liked flashiness and wasn't quite ready to leave it behind.

"Why do you ask?" Luke said.

"I mean I'm just saying with all that's been going on, maybe you're moving too fast."

"Nessa, let me worry about all of that."

"But…"

"End of subject."

"I hate when you do that shit, Luke," Nessa fired back.

"What shit?"

"When you shut me down like that. I'm a grown ass woman, Luke. I'm twenty-three, and I have just as much right to voice my opinion and thoughts regarding this relationship as you do."

"I didn't say you didn't."

"Might as well when you say end of subject like I'm your child or something. You won't even let me have a say so in which house we move into."

"Nessa…"

"And what about marriage?"

"Nessa, we're not having this conversation. I've already told you I don't want to talk about marriage now."

"Well, I want to talk about it. You keep blowing me off each and every time I bring it up."

Nessa had brought up the subject of marriage countless times before. Each time, Luke shut her down.

"Nessa…"

"Luke, I love you. Why can't we get married?"

"Nessa…"

"Why does it always have to be…?"

"Goddamn it, Nessa!" Luke yelled through the phone.

Nessa's body jolted at the sound. Luke had never yelled at her before.

"I said we're not talking about marriage any time soon! I'm not getting married!" Luke continued. "Now, I let you go on your little tirade for the past several minutes. I let you get things off your chest. Enough is enough. I said what I meant and the shit's final!"

The phone went dead.

Holding the phone in her hand, Nessa was shocked

that Luke screamed at her. But besides shocked, she was filled with anger. She wanted to be more to Luke than just his girlfriend. She wanted a ring. She wanted a huge wedding.

She wanted to be his wife.

"You okay?" Trinity asked.

"I'm good," Nessa lied.

Nessa put on her cover-up and headed back into the house. As she headed by the foyer with things on her mind, she glanced out and saw a UPS truck at the gate. Security was accepting a package. Remembering the call from her father, and knowing she couldn't take a chance on the package ending up in the wrong hands, Nessa dashed out and down the drive way. "Did something come for me?" she asked the bodyguard.

"Yeah," he answered.

"Why didn't anyone tell me?"

Before he could say anything else, Nessa snatched the envelope from him and quickly made her way back to the house. As she did, she had a strong idea of what was on the video. Her hands trembled as she held the envelope. Reaching the house, she opened the door and nearly stumbled backwards when she saw Chetti standing there.

"Since when do you start getting mail here?" Chetti asked.

Nessa was caught off guard. She didn't quite know what to say.

"I asked you a damn question."

"It was important."

"I don't give fuck how important it is. This isn't your house."

"Chetti, it's just a piece of mail. It's not a big deal."

Stepping towards Nessa, Chetti said, "In my house, I decide what a big deal is and what a big deal isn't."

136

Fed up, Nessa attempted to brush past Chetti.

"Bitch, what's in that envelope?" Chetti asked, grabbing hold of Nessa's arm.

Snatching away, Nessa said, "None of your damn business."

"Who the hell do you think you're talking to?"

"*Your* old ass!"

"Bitch, I will wipe the floor with your trashy ass."

"Then make a move!"

Chetti's eyes narrowed.

Nessa looked Chetti directly into her eyes. "Out of respect for Luke, I back down from you but I'm not doing that shit anymore. Disrespect will be met with disrespect, bitch."

Nessa then stormed off.

Fuming, Chetti muttered to herself, "Muthafuckas around here have forgotten who the queen bitch is. Muthafuckas have tried me one time too many times. I think it's time I remind their asses."

Ignoring Chetti and her mutterings, Nessa ascended the staircase and headed to the bedroom with the envelope in her hand. Reaching the room, she locked the door, ripped open the envelope and pulled out a CD. Seconds later, she slid it into the computer to watch. Several moments later, her stomach sank at what she saw.

"I hate you," she whispered, speaking of her father and knowing his intentions were to tear her down if she didn't satisfy him. "I fucking hate you."

Tears streamed down her face, then dripped from her chin as Nessa thought about how her father never truly loved her. He only seemed to love himself and it showed through his constant actions.

Chapter 14

The Five Points Mall in Accokeek, MD was going to be the largest shopping mall in not only the entire state of Maryland, but also several of the states nearby. It would house four floors, each of its hundreds of leasing spaces already leased. On its lot surrounding it would be a Walmart, Office Depot, and several restaurants. The price tag for the entire development would be several hundred million dollars. But considering the fortune it would bring in, it would be worth the investment.

In a tailor-made Italian suit and loafers, Luke sat at the far end of the conference room table staring out the picture window at McPherson Square in downtown D.C. Leaning back in the leather of the high-back chair, he was silent and in deep thought as he awaited Pamela Benson, one of the co-investors of the Five Points Mall. Sitting in the first chair along the right side of the conference table in a three-piece Gucci suit was Eric Thomas, Luke's personal business attorney. For the moment, he was silent also while going through paperwork to pass the time as he and his client awaited Ms. Benson.

Luke's mind was being pulled in several different

directions as he stared out over the city. He could still hear and see the gunshot that killed his own son. He could still see Gavin lying on the grime covered floor of that warehouse pleading with all his heart to be put out of his misery. The memory sent aches and pains through Luke's heart along with heavy regret. He wished with everything inside him that things could've been different for his son. But no matter how much he wished, reality was still what it was and Gavin was still dead.

Luke's thoughts were also on his mother heavily. He loved her but there was no way around admitting the obvious…

She was a cruel cold-hearted bitch.

With his own eyes, Luke had watched his mother do evil things to people, sometimes just because she could. She was a woman who reveled in hurting people and rubbing their faces in the fact that she had power and money beyond most of their imaginations. She thrived on tearing lives apart. It seemed to be what she'd lived for. Luke hated that. He hated what she seemed to stand for. But no matter how much he hated her, there was one thing he hated more…

The fact that he went along with her cruel acts.

One act in particular that brought shame to Luke was the betrayal of his brother Cedrick. That was one act he could never bring himself to think about. In fact, the current moment was the first time he'd thought about it in a year.

So strange, Luke thought to himself. So strange to be living in the same house with a brother you *never* see, you never *wish* to see, you choose *not* to see. What type of family operates that way? What type of brothers have that type of relationship or lack of?

Mr. Bishop had left sixty-one percent of the family's

fortune and operations to Cedrick, a Harvard graduate with ambitions to take the family out of the streets and position them in the upper echelons of legitimate Corporate America. The remaining thirty-nine percent was to be distributed evenly amongst Chetti, Luke and Darien. Considering Trinity his princess and not wanting to place her in harm's way, Mr. Bishop left her money but forbade her involvement in the family business.

Chills now ran down Luke's spine at the memories of how vicious the arguments between Chetti and Cedrick were. They were knock down drag out as Cedrick fought hard to shift the family's interests from the streets to Corporate America. He was passionate about it very much so but Chetti was just as passionate about keeping the family firmly planted in the only genre of business it had ever known.

It wasn't long before Chetti realized the power struggle between her and her son would tear the family apart. She called a meeting between her, Luke and Darien. In the meeting, she convinced her sons that Cedrick's plans for the family would destroy all that had been worked for and he had to be stopped. Although loving their brother, they took their mother's side and were in agreement. So with the promise of each of them gaining 33% of the family's business, they went along with whatever she had in mind to take away Cedrick's power.

One night while in his sleep, Chetti had Cedrick kidnapped. He was taken to a basement, tied to a chair, blindfolded and pumped with drugs several times a day for months. Over time, the drugs; ferociously addictive, turned his brain to mush. They took away his connection to reality. During those months, Trinity had been told that Cedrick had been killed. Cedrick was then brought back to the family compound, locked in a bedroom in an unused wing, and held captive ever since.

Now sitting at the conference table, Luke shook his head at the memory. He'd betrayed his younger brother. It was the brother he'd once looked up to. The one he'd shared dreams and ideas with…the one he'd wanted to be just like. He felt horrible.

Ironically, Luke was now following in his brother's footsteps. It was now his intentions to take the family corporate. He was now just as passionate about it as his brother once was. Realizing that, Luke knew if his mother would be heartless enough to lock away one son to keep control of the family, he had no doubt she would do something similar or even worse to him.

Luke had to do something about his mother. He had no choice. It was definite. He loved her. But if there was only one thing he'd ever learned from her, it was eat or be eaten.

Luke chose to eat.

With his mind made up, there was still worry about what would have to be done regarding Darien. Darien and Chetti were kindred spirits. They both had bloody mouths and relished the streets. Luke knew Darien would *never* go against their mother. How would he deal with him?

The door to the conference room opened. Pamela Benson, a beautiful thirty-five year old white woman in a pleated Marc Jacobs skirt and studded blouse, appeared with her assistant. The two of them were carrying briefcases.

"Please forgive my tardiness," she said to Luke and Eric while making her way alongside the table to shake their hands. "Traffic from the airport was horrific."

"Promptness is a virtue," Eric scolded with his eyes. He ignored the hand Pamela extended his way.

"Not a problem," Luke told her, now standing, attempting to lighten Eric's comment.

Ms. Benson and her young personal assistant sat down and placed their briefcases beside their feet.

"May I get you ladies anything?" Luke asked as he sat back down, grinning way too hard.

Pamela shook her head. "No, thank you."

"Then I guess it's on to business," Eric stated quickly.

Both men placed their hands on the table top and folded them waiting for Pamela to speak.

"I have good news and bad news, Mr. Bishop," Pamela informed.

Luke looked at his co-investor. He always admired her beauty. Her bleached blonde hair, made thin from too many years of hair dye, was parted down the middle with beautiful beach waves. Standing at 5'9 with smooth ivory skin, piercing blue eyes and small perky breast, she could've easily been a model.

"Okay," Luke finally said.

"The good news is that my partners and I have agreed to take you on as a co-investor in the Five Points Mall deal."

"Great."

"The bad news is your individual investment will have to be fifty million instead of the agreed thirty million."

Luke frowned. "Wow…steep number."

"And one that sounds highly elevated," Eric added.

"Yes, but my partners and I can't feel comfortable bringing you aboard on this project for a penny less," Pamela advised.

"I understand."

"So, do we have a deal?"

"Absolutely not," Eric interjected , pushing himself

away from the table. "Luke, I think we need to talk, alone."

"Hold tight, Eric. I got this," he said with his hand formed in mid-air in stop position. Luke thought for a moment. Fifty million dollars was a lot of money to invest. He hadn't been planning on that amount.

"I assure you, Mr. Bishop, this is an investment opportunity that someone else will jump on immediately if you don't. We already have several suitable investors inquiring about the project. Whether with them or with you, my partners and I are ready to move forward with construction immediately after all signatures have been placed to paper."

Pamela's assistant pushed the new paperwork in Eric's direction. "All of the numbers and justifications are there in black and white," she informed.

Eric didn't even bother to grab the papers. He simply shook his head with frustration.

Luke didn't want to take a chance on losing out on the opportunity. Without knowing where all the money would come from, he finally said, "We've got a deal."

Nessa paced back and forth across the bedroom floor. She'd been doing so for the past several hours. She just couldn't sit still. She couldn't stop moving no matter how hard she tried. She was even crying. The contents of the video had her that way.

Nessa was on the verge of losing everything including her life. The contents of the video could be her Death Certificate. Realizing that possibility had her sweating and on edge.

Why couldn't her father just leave things alone, Nessa wondered. Why couldn't he just let her live her life?

Hadn't he exposed her to enough as a kid? Hadn't he had enough of a negative impact and influence on her? Why couldn't he just let her go?

Sitting on the bed and worriedly dropping her face into her hands, Nessa saw Luke's face in her mind. She remembered Trinity telling her earlier how vicious Luke could be, how murderous he could be. Chills ran down Nessa's spine as she admitted to herself how much she would deserve to die by Luke's hand for what she'd done in her past. Raising her face from her hands, she grabbed the mouse, clicked a button and watched the video once again on the screen.

"Ahhhhhhhhhhhhhhhh!" the man screamed horrifically while tied to a chair completely naked.

"Where's the money?" Mrs. Kingston, Nessa's mother, asked as she pulled the blowtorch's flame away from his chest.

"Fuck you!" he screamed. "You'll never see a fuckin' *penny* of my damn money!"

Mrs. Kingston placed the blowtorch to his stomach. "Ahhhhhhhhhhhhhhhhhhhhhhhhhh!"

The man rocked wildly back and forth in the chair in reaction to the pain. He gritted his teeth.

"You owe me, muthafucka!"

"Bitch, I don't owe you shit!"

The blowtorch was placed to his arm.

"Oh, God, ahhhhhhhhhhhhhhhhhhhhhhhhhhhhh!"

The stench of burning flesh filled the basement.

"You think I'm playing wit' yo' ass?"

"Fuck you, Piper!"

More burning.

More screaming.

As the torture took place, another person; a seventeen year old girl, stood by covering her nose and mouth to avoid the foul smell. She didn't even watch although her own father had subjected her to watching many murders he'd committed himself over the years.

The girl's name?

Nessa.

"Nessa, come get some of this," Mrs. Kingston ordered. "Come burn this nigga!"

Nessa shook her head. She had agreed to help her mother set the man up for extortion. But she hadn't agreed to participate in his torture. And she for damn sure hadn't agreed to video the act.

"Come on, girl. Come burn his ass!"

"Ma, he's not going to give us the money."

"He'll give it up."

"Ma, let's just…"

More burning.

"Ahhhhhhhhhhhhhhhhhhhhhhhhhhhhhhhh!"

The man's screams made Nessa cringe. She'd never heard a human being scream like that.

"You gonna pay up, muthafucka?"

"Fuck you, bitch. Piper, I swear, when my family finds out about this, your ass is as good as dead!"

Piper had had enough. Tossing the blowtorch, she pulled out a .38 Revolver and aimed it at his head. "I'm done playin' wit' yo' ass. Give me the money or I'll blow yo' head off."

Sweating and in tremendous agony, he looked directly up into Mrs. Kingston's eyes and said, "Do it, hoe. What the fuck you waitin' on?"

She cocked the hammer.

Nessa tensed.

"Where's the money?"

"Fuck you. Kill me, bitch. Kill me!"

CRACK!!!!!

Squeezing the trigger, Piper sent a bullet through his kneecap.

"Ahhhhhhhhhhhhhhhh, you fuckin' bitch!" he screamed in torment. He began breathing hard and fast to deal with the pain.

"Where's the money!"

"Go to hell!"

CRACK!!!!!

Another bullet tore through his other kneecap.

Amidst the screams, Nessa held her arms around herself. She hoped the moment would end soon. She hadn't signed on for this.

Placing the gun to the man's temple, Piper said, "This is it. Sign everything over as you promised you lying sack of shit! And give me my money! Or you die right here and now, nigga!"

Closing his eyes and tensing his body, he said, "Do it, bitch, because you're not getting a single dime out of me. I don't let muthafuckas like you extort me. I do the extorting, bitch!"

"I gave up everything for you, nigga!" she said, getting choked up. "I allowed my husband to think I was possibly dead just to be with you. I stayed out of my daughter's life for four years to be with you! Do you know what that shit felt like? Do you know what it did to our relationship?"

"AND…" he snapped sarcastically.

Fresh out of patience, Piper tucked the gun and pulled out a box cutter. Before the man could respond, with one swipe, she opened his throat from ear to ear. Blood spewed and sprayed as the back of his skull fell against the back of the chair. His eyes rolled up into his head as he struggled to breathe. The more he tried, the more he began to drown in his own blood.

Filthy Rich BY: KENDALL BANKS

With trembling hands, Nessa clicked the off button on the screen and turned off the computer. Once again, she dropped her head. She felt stressed beyond belief. She stood and walked over to the window. God, how she wished she wouldn't have let her mother talk her into being an accomplice to that man's death.

Once again, Luke's face appeared in Nessa's mind. She and he were connected by the circumstances of that video. Their lives were connected at that moment without either of them knowing. They were connected through the man her mother, Mrs. Piper Kingston had murdered.

His name?

Mr. Bishop.

Mr. Bishop had been the love of Piper's life for years. They built a life together where she helped him climb the ranks. Every dollar he earned, she'd helped in some way. She'd taken lots of heat for him too, even a bullet once. He'd used her name to legitimize certain deals; all with the promise that she'd be rewarded in the end. It didn't matter that she had a child, Nessa that wasn't his. It didn't even matter that she was estranged from her husband. The two were madly in love. Piper had given him her all.

Unfortunately, Mr. Bishop had been married to Chetti all along , and was pretty much living a double life. Mr. Bishop's cheating and betrayal eventually caught up with him after years of plying two house-holds. Chetti found out, and soon, all that Piper thought was hers was soon stripped from her; houses, cars, jewelry, and cash. She was left with nothing.

No pride.

No money.

No place to go.

With revenge deep in her heart she hoped that one

day she'd claim what was hers. Sadly, even death couldn't get back all the material possessions and love she'd lost. He died without signing a thing.

Staring out into the night, Nessa couldn't stop her body from shaking. Her father, through his own blind greed, was now unknowingly throwing a monkey wrench in her plans. He was jeopardizing everything for a few measly dollars. She shook her head. Turning from the window, she headed back to the bed, and grabbed the envelope the CD had been mailed in. Once again, she read the note it had come with.

Meet me at the park tomorrow. If you don't, I will make sure your boyfriend sees this *personally*.

Crumpling the note, Nessa knew she had no choice. Until she could figure out how to deal with her father, she had to pacify him.

Nessa's phone notified her of an incoming text.

Grabbing her phone, Nessa pulled up the text and saw it was from Brandon. "Shit," she said, realizing she'd forgotten about tonight.

YOU'RE LATE, the text read.

Trying to get out of the house, she returned lying.

Try HARDER. Trust me; I'm not the type of man you want to stand up.

The final text made Nessa nervous. She was getting in far too deep on all fronts. "Fuck!" she yelled in frustration while banging her fists against the sides of her head.

Silence.

Seconds passed as she buried her head into the crisp linen.

More silence.

Finally, Nessa grabbed her phone again and texted back to Brandon "I'm On My Way."

Knowing she couldn't afford to piss Brandon off,

Nessa got up from the bed and began to get dressed. As she did, another text came through. Figuring it was Brandon, Nessa grabbed the phone and opened the text. Immediately she realized it wasn't from Brandon.

A solemn expression appeared on Nessa's face at the message and the name of the sender, both reminders of her past, both reminders of what she was doing in the Bishop family mansion. She plopped back down to the bed again and sat in silence while staring at the text but no longer reading it.

Last Shot. Been texting yo ass 4 the last couple of days. Don't make me show my ass. Call me or I'm showin up at the Bishop camp tonight. Guns blazing, bitch! Do your JOB.

Nessa was in no hurry to return the text or call. It didn't matter that the sender of the text was…

Her mother.

Chapter 15

It took a lot of ducking, camouflaging and creeping for Nessa to get out of the house and off its grounds unnoticed. Since the drive-by at the funeral, security had tightened drastically. The guards, each of them heavily armed, were watching all movements in and outside the gates closely. And there was no doubt they would kill if they had to.

Having to leave her car behind, Nessa sat in a cab with a lot on her mind as the driver maneuvered his way underneath the night's darkness. Nessa was stressed, especially after receiving her mother's text. She hadn't returned her call although she knew she would have to before the end of the night. For now though, she had other things on her mind.

Nessa had gotten tired of being passive. She was tired of being the peace maker; it wasn't really her make-up to begin with. She'd been trained to be ruthless and to take whatever she wanted. The back and forth with Luke over the phone was the first chink in her armor, the first bit of exposure to the woman she really was. The back and forth with Chetti was the next. Now it was time to let it all hang out.

Nessa knew she had to get a grip on the situation she was in. She'd been patient enough. Her patience, though, had gotten her in too deep. Her father and Brandon were both threatening her, taking her kindness for weakness. If she was going to control both situations with the men, she was going to have to show them the type of vicious bitch she really was.

And then of course there was her mother…BAD ASS, PIPER, who'd shank her grandmother if she had to. She knew Piper expected her to accomplish what she'd signed up for. They'd had gone to great measures to have Mook and Nessa show up at Luke's favorite restaurant the day they first met. Mook got paid well, and Piper was still waiting for her big pay off…The BISHOP Fortune.

"This street right here," Nessa told the driver. "Turn right here."

The driver did as he was told.

The neighborhood Nessa was now being chauffeured through was one of the 'hoods her father had terrorized back in the day. She had basically grown up in it. It had been a while since she had been back though.

"Slow up a lil bit," Nessa told the driver as she looked out the window squinting to see the addresses on the run down houses that lined the right side of the dark street, a street that had already been on two episodes of *The First 48* this year.

The driver slowed the taxi. Its brakes squeaked as it began to crawl down the side street at almost a snail's pace.

Nessa watched house after house pass by; some abandoned, others looking as if they *should* be abandoned.

Growing nervous at his surroundings and fearing getting robbed, the driver said, "Ma'am, are you sure this is the street?" The uneasiness was evident in his voice.

"Yeah," she returned.

"Ma'am, most of these houses are abandoned."

"Wowwww, a bitch can't put anything over on yo' ass. How'd you know?" She shook her head.

He didn't respond to her sarcasm.

Knowing the driver was scared, Nessa pulled two hundred dollars out of her purse and handed it over the seat to him. "If I wanted you robbed, I'd be *taking* your money, not *giving* you money."

He stuffed the money in his pocket and kept driving slowly.

Spotting the address she was looking for, Nessa said, "This is the house. Stop right here."

The driver slammed on the brakes.

Tossing him another fifty dollars, Nessa said, "Wait right here. I'll be back out in a minute."

Nessa hopped out of the car in an Alexander Mc-Queen skirt and five-inch heels. Looking too high-priced for a neighborhood like this, she made her way up the decrepit walkway towards the house. After stepping foot on its porch, she knocked.

Seconds passed.

Nessa looked up and down the street.

The door finally opened.

A female appeared, not a feminine one though. She was a stud. Her hair was in thick cornrows that draped down her back. A tattooed teardrop was underneath the outer corner of her left eye. Tattoos ran down her arms. She wore a sports bra, sagging jean shorts, white socks and a pair of Adidas flip-flops.

Her name was Juicy. She was NaNa's road dog.

"You got that for me?" Nessa asked.

"Yeah, but NaNa wanted to handle you personally."

At that very moment, an over-sized man who was black as tar, said, "Damn girl, I see you got yo'self in a little trouble. You sho' you just need one?"

"Yeah."

"A'ight, come on back."

Nessa walked to the back of the house to see NaNa's latest dime piece, a young white girl in only a pair of panties, lying on the couch watching an episode of *Scandal*. On the table in front of her was a bottle of Peach Ciroc, a gun and a small pile of weed. In her mouth was a Swisher Sweet stuffed with Kush. She didn't bat an eye at Nessa.

As silence filled the room, Juicy headed toward a cabinet, her flip-flops making swishing sounds across the cheap and stained carpet. Seconds later, she returned with a small box. In it was a brand new 9mm. Glock. Handing it to Nessa, she said, "Fresh off the truck. Ain't got no bodies on it or nothin'."

As Nessa opened the box and pulled the gun out, NaNa told Juicy, and the white chick to clear the room. Sitting the box down, Nessa held the gun with both hands and aimed at a nearby wall making sure the barrel was straight like a seasoned assassin. Satisfied, she asked, "Got some hollow tips?"

"Of course."

"Let me get some."

"I got you."

NaNa headed to another room and returned a couple seconds later with a box of hollow-tipped bullets. As he handed them to Nessa, he said, "Looks like you've got intentions to smoke a muthafucka."

Nessa didn't answer verbally. She only nodded.

"You know if you need me, holler. We go too far back. I got some shit that'll light four muthafuckas up at one time."

Nessa laughed then smiled. She was happy to know if she ever needed help, NaNa had her back.

"Damnnnn," she stated. "No need for all that. This is good for now."

Finally, fed up with her father's threats, Nessa was ready to kill him at their meeting the next morning. She had far too much on the line to take a chance on him fucking things up. Also, Brandon was making too many waves. He'd have to go, too. Realizing both men needed to meet their maker, that's what prompted Nessa to call NaNa, the militant gun dealer she'd known for years.

Now stuffing the gun back into the box, Nessa paid NaNa and dapped him up. Moments later, she was in the back seat of the cab stuffing the gun's clip full of bullets as the taxi made its way downtown to the hotel where Nessa was to meet Brandon. As she did, she texted Sidra to let her know exactly where she was going just in case things didn't quite turn out the way she planned. If Brandon somehow got the drop on her, she wanted it to be well-known to Luke and the cops that Brandon was the very last person to see her alive.

As usual, Brandon's hands were all over Nessa. He was kissing her all over her body while pawing and grabbing her body parts like a pervert. As he did, she could smell cigarettes and liquor on his breath. She could tell he was drunk. "You like that, baby?" he asked slurring in his words. "You want this dick?"

Nessa rolled her eyes. *God, how in the world had she let shit go this far*, she wondered?

"Do you?" he asked, looking her in the eyes.

"Yeah," she answered dryly while glancing at her ten thousand dollar Hermes bag sitting on a table across the room. She couldn't wait to see the look on Brandon's face when she shoved the gun into his temple.

Seeing that she wasn't interested, Brandon asked, "What's wrong?"

"What's *wrong*?" she repeated his question while looking at him like he was crazy. "Nigga, you're the side dick. You know that. But you're making threats to me like you're my man. Fuck you mean what's wrong?"

Backing away and shaking his head, Brandon grabbed a half empty bottle of Gin from a nearby table and took a swig. "Your priorities are fucked up."

"What do you mean?"

"I mean you're focused on the wrong things, the wrong man."

Nessa had no idea what he was talking about. She figured the alcohol had him just rambling on.

"Nessa, Luke's days are numbered."

"What are you talking about?"

"He's a drug dealer, Nessa. Drug dealers don't retire. They don't walk away from the game Scott-free. In the end, baby, they all go down."

Nessa couldn't believe Brandon was saying these things about his own cousin. Whether they were true or not, Brandon wasn't supposed to be speaking on his own flesh and blood like that.

With the bottle still in his hand, Brandon returned to Nessa and wrapped his arms around her. His breath smelled atrocious. "You need a man like me," he told her. "A man with a damn good job. A man who doesn't have to spend his days looking over his damn shoulder."

"A man like you, huh?" she asked uninterested.

"Yeah, a man like me."

Nessa fought hard to keep from gagging at the stench coming from Brandon's mouth. His breath smelled like hot garbage. This was a far cry from the day she originally fucked him.

"Nessa, open your eyes. Luke doesn't love you. He's not capable of loving anyone. Yea, I know he's brought you to the house to live with him, and is filling your head with all these wonderful dreams and plans. But, sweetheart, trust and believe you're not the first."

Nessa was now listening to him.

"You're not even the only woman he's fucking. He's got bitches all over the fucking place."

Hearing Brandon tell those lies pissed Nessa off. She couldn't believe he was going this far just to get some pussy. She knew Brandon wanted her for himself but damn. Brandon's lies had her ready to grab her purse, dip into the bathroom, cock the gun and come ready to place a bullet in his head.

"You don't believe me, huh?" he asked.

"No."

Shaking his head, Brandon stepped back from Nessa, pulled out his cell phone and pulled up a pic. Showing Nessa the screen, he said, "See what I'm saying?"

There was a photo of a stylish woman of Persian decent with one arm wrapped around Luke and the other clutching his exposed dick. The grin on his face was clearly visible.

"That fucka!" Nessa exclaimed with anger.

Brandon grinned then exposed the next photo.

"Now look at this shit!"

At that moment, Nessa saw a pic of Luke hugging a white woman. There was then another pic of him kissing her. Seeing the pics sent shudders of anger through Nessa.

"I told you," Brandon uttered. "He's just stringing

you along. From what I'm hearing lately, he's been spending a whole lot of time with this one in particular. He really likes her."

Nessa seethed.

She thought back to the beating she'd taken by his goons. She thought about the dirt being poured on top of her while in that casket. The trauma she'd suffered still haunted her at night. She was willing to die for him. She had ducked her mother for months with thoughts of botching her plans. After all, she truly loved Luke.

"Sorry, Nessa, but you're just temporary. You just house booty." He laughed. "Good, juicy booty, I might add, though."

Snatching away from Brandon, Nessa walked to the opposite side of the room and thought for a moment. She was now seeing red. Here she was supposed to be playing Luke. But come to find out he was playing her. She knew she wasn't supposed to get caught up in feelings. Her love for Luke was supposed to be just an act but obviously she'd allowed herself to really fall for him. It was truly obvious now.

She wanted revenge.

Coming up with a solution for how she could deal with her father without having to do it herself, Nessa turned, headed back towards Brandon and got lost in his arms. She sighed and began to manufacture tears. "Thank you, Brandon, for being the only one in your family to care enough about me to tell the truth."

"It's okay, baby."

Placing her hand over Brandon's crotch and squeezing softly, she told him, "Everyone just keeps wanting to take advantage of me."

"What do you mean?"

"First my father. Now Luke."

"Your father? What do you mean?"

"He's trying to extort money from me."

"Why?"

"He knows Luke has money. He's threatening to kill me if I don't come meet him tomorrow. I know he'll do it."

Nessa put on her best act as the tears streamed down her face. Her lips were quivering. As she acted, she made sure to squeeze and rub Brandon's crotch. She could feel it grow and harden in his pants.

"I'll go with you," Brandon said.

"No, Brandon. I don't want you to get involved. He's dangerous."

Taking Nessa's face into his hands, he told her, "Nessa, I'm going with you. I'm going to handle him for you."

"What do you mean by *handle*?"

"I'll tell his ass to back the fuck off."

"That won't work. I've tried that."

Releasing Nessa, he pulled out his gun and told her, "I'll kill him then."

Wanting her father dead but scared it could possibly come back to her, Nessa replied, "I would much rather see his ass in prison. He's always telling me he wants to connect with Luke and the family somehow. Maybe we could set him up or something?"

Brandon placed the gun at his side. "Yeah, we could do that."

"Thanks for having my back, baby," Nessa said as she pulled close to Brandon again still fighting to keep from gagging at the smell of his breath.

"Don't worry about it."

"Baby, I'm sorry for not believing you when you first told me about Luke."

"It's alright, sweetheart. I understand."

Nessa kissed him. The taste of his tongue made her want to puke. She held tough though. "Brandon, do you think me and you can work out?"

"Of course. We'll have to stay low key for a minute. But in time, we'll be good."

A text came through Brandon's phone. Looking at it, he smiled. "Speak of the devil."

"What?" Nessa asked.

"Just like I said, in time we'll be good. Won't be too much time though. Got a meeting set up with the L.A. crew that's out for Luke's head tomorrow afternoon."

"About what?"

"Can't tell you all of that."

"Well, I want to go."

Brandon frowned. "Hell no. Are you crazy?"

"Brandon, after the way Luke played me, if this has anything to do with him getting his ass paid back for breaking my heart, I want to see it."

"Nessa, this is for big dogs."

Nessa pulled herself close to Brandon again and placed her hand over his crotch. Beginning to kiss him around the neck, she begged, "Please, Brandon. Please, baby. Please let me go."

Brandon grew weak at Nessa's kisses. His dick grew hard inside his pants.

"I have to be a part of this, Brandon. Please, baby."

Nessa's grasps and grips on Brandon became wild and aggressive. Her kisses became sloppy.

"Nessa…"

At that moment, thoughts of why she'd been attracted to Brandon in the first place filled her. She ripped open Brandon's shirt and began to plant kisses all over his chest. She then began to suck on his nipple.

"Shittttttttt, Nessa," he moaned.

159

While continuing to kiss him, she unzipped his pants and stuffed her hands inside. Stroking his dick, she pleaded again, "Baby, please let me go."

"Nessa, I..."

Nessa dropped to her knees and began to deep throat Brandon intensely. As she made slurping and gagging sounds on his thick penis, she looked up innocently into his eyes. Nessa was good at being a manipulator and knew her dick sucking skills were on point.

Meanwhile, Brandon couldn't keep his eyes from rolling up into his head. His moans and groans became louder with each of Nessa's tongue strokes. "Yesssssssss, oooooohhhhhh, yeahhhhhhh. Suck it girl, suck it."

Without warning, Brandon gripped the back of Nessa's head forcing her to go deeper. Like a good girl, Nessa began bobbing on the dick, sending Brandon into a frenzy.

She devoured him.

He made crazy hissing sounds.

Ten minutes later he was cumming. He finally broke down and gave Nessa what she wanted...

"Alright, baby, you can go with me."

It was a little after eleven p.m. when Nessa hopped back into another cab. So much had changed in her life over the past twenty-four hours; most of which she wasn't sure how to handle. She still had too much on her mind. The only thing that helped to ease her thoughts was the fact that she now had Brandon in the palm of her hand. As long as she fucked him good like she did tonight and strung him along, she could now count on him to tell her anything she needed to know. It was also obvious he was going to play a huge part in Nessa's plan to eventually take over the family.

"Kinda late for a pretty young lady to be out, don't 'cha think?"

"I'm paying you to drive, not think," Nessa shot back as the cab driver turned the corner.

He just gawked at Nessa as she whipped her phone from her purse to call her mother. It was the call she dreaded. As it rang, it seemed like an eternity before she answered.

"Long time no hear," her mother answered.

"I know, Ma. Things been hectic."

"Hectic my ass. You had a job to do…and you failed. Do I need to step in?"

Nessa's heart raced. "No, Ma. I got this. I was trying to get Luke to marry me."

"Marry you? Bitch, are you crazy! You used to be a tough, rugged bitch. Now you all soft and shit, looking for love. Well, it don't exist. Believe that! Put that fairy tale shit behind you and take care of Luke, his brother and his mother. You hear me?"

The words she spoke made it clear to Nessa that Piper meant business.

"We meeting up tomorrow. Just me and you, doll. Wait for my call for a location." Before Nessa could object the line went dead.

It didn't take long for Nessa to walk the dark road and ease her way back into the house after being let through the gates. The guards definitely thought it was highly suspicious that she'd walked home. Nessa hoped like hell they didn't alert Luke.

Softly closing the front door, she held her heels in her hand and walked quietly to the staircase. Reaching it, she headed to the second floor, tip-toeing, hoping not to wake anybody up. Although mostly quiet, stark noses could be heard once Nessa neared her bedroom. She paused in the hallway attempting to capture the direction of the sounds.

The halls were silent and still.

Yet still, there was that loud, knocking sound.

Unsure where the noises where coming from, she eventually headed toward that strange room on the opposite end of the mansion. She'd meant to ask Brandon if he knew anything about the room, but she'd forgotten. Thinking about the room, Nessa now made her way through the halls, with her heels in hand. Finally reaching the hall where the room was located, she could hear voices and sounds. Who could've been up? She wondered. Maybe it was Trinity? She figured it wasn't Darien since he rarely came home before the sun came up.

As she approached the room, the voices and sounds grew louder and louder. When she reached the room, Nessa noticed that door was cracked. Stepping towards it, Nessa pushed it open slightly. What she saw made her gasp.

"Fuck your mother good, Cedrick," Chetti moaned. Naked, she was straddling a man in a chair. His strong, muscular looking back was to the door while Chetti was facing the door. Her head was raised in pleasure and her eyes were closed. "Fuck your mother, baby."

Nessa's bottom jaw dropped. She couldn't believe what she saw.

"Ohhhhhh, God, Cedrick," Chetti moaned to the ceiling. Her body was soaked in sweat as her low cut shirt hung off her shoulders. "Fuck momma with your big dick. Fuck your mother's pussy."

Nessa's face twisted into something far beyond disbelief. She was actually seeing Chetti fucking her own son, a son who was supposed to be dead. The shit was *crazy*.

"That's a good boy," Chetti said with pleasure as she rode her son's dick wildly, making sure to take every single inch of it inside her. As she dug her nails into his back, she drew blood while the force of her body against his was causing the bottoms of the chair's legs to scrape loudly back and forth across the floor's surface.

Nessa watched in silence while shaking her head at times. She wanted to turn away. She wanted to leave but something wouldn't let her. She could only stand there with her mouth wide open.

Finally getting her orgasm, Chetti climbed up off of Cedrick. Still naked, she made her way across the bedroom to grab her clothes and put her pants back on. As she did, Nessa pulled back slightly and blended with the hallway's darkness to avoid being seen.

While getting dressed, Chetti told Cedrick, "Look at you. Used to be the heir to a dynasty. You had the world in your hands. Now you're nothing but a piece of dick."

Nessa listened.

"It was *you* who made this decision. It was *you* who made me do this to you. All you had to do was play ball."

Cedrick said nothing. He simply stared off into space in absolute silence. His pajama pants and underwear were down to his ankles but his erection was gone.

Shaking her head while continuing to get dressed, Chetti continued, "Now your damn brother Luke has got the same backwards thoughts and pipedreams you had. Looks like I'm going to have to get another room ready, huh?"

Nessa listened closely to every word.

"Ungrateful children," Chetti added. Her eyes then looked across the room at the door.

Nessa backed away quickly hoping she hadn't been

seen. Chetti's footsteps could be heard stammering toward the door. Nearly stumbling over her feet, Nessa quickly dashed down the hall. Finally reaching her bedroom, she ran inside, locked the door and jumped in bed beneath the covers unable to forget what she'd just seen and heard.

For minutes, she waited to even move an inch of her body. Both eyes watched the bottom of the doorway, hoping Chetti wouldn't come her way. As minutes passed, Nessa finally decided to reach over to grab her phone. Nervously, she dialed Luke's number.

"C'mon Luke, answer, baby, answer."

Her eyes remained locked on the bedroom door.

Then…

Of course Luke's voicemail picked up.

"Luke, where the fuck are you?" she whispered. "I need you to come get me."

Filthy Rich BY: KENDALL BANKS

Chapter 16

Nessa had seen a lot in life, more than most folks she knew. She'd witnessed murders. She'd witnessed violence. She'd seen brutality. But she'd never witnessed anything like what she had seen between Chetti and Cedrick. It was now half past 9:00 a.m. and she couldn't get it out of her head. She hadn't even been able to sleep more than an hour before what she'd seen would manifest itself in her dreams. Each time, she'd wake up in a cold sweat.

Throughout the night, Nessa tried calling Luke over and over again. She'd called him at least a dozen times. Each time though her call went directly to voicemail. Spite brewed inside her during those calls. She wondered if he was out with that white bitch. She wondered if he was inside her. She wondered if he was lying beside her while holding her in his arms. The possibility pissed Nessa off.

Despite her anger towards Luke, Nessa still always found herself going back to what she'd seen last night. The shit was the absolute creepiest scene she could imagine. It was straight out of one of those *Lifetime* movies.

With her door still locked and the morning sun having been up for a few hours now, Nessa sat in her bed quietly while thinking. She wondered how the hell a mother could have sex with her own son. But more importantly, she wondered how a mother could make the world think her son was dead.

"*Fuck your mother, Cedrick*," Chetti's words played themselves inside Nessa's head. Hearing them and seeing the memory made her stomach jerk. She gagged. "*Fuck your mother good.*"

Nessa couldn't hold back. She leapt from the bed, dashed to the bathroom and threw up in the toilet. After emptying her stomach and then sitting beside the toilet dry heaving for a while, she brushed her teeth and went back to the bedroom.

Nessa had no idea what to do. It was only now that she realized Luke must've been in on Cedrick's captivity. He *had* to. The mansion was huge but there was no fuckin' way he could be living there for this amount of time and not know his brother was being held in that room. That was why he kept telling Nessa that the room was just a place where Chetti kept quote unquote "Old Things."

The lies.

The secrets.

Both Trinity and Brandon had warned Nessa about family secrets and how dangerous things could become for her if she discovered those secrets or inquired about them.

"*These walls have ears. They hear everything,*" Trinity's words played in Nessa's ears and mind. "*Asking questions can get you killed.*"

Remembering what Trinity told her, Nessa grabbed her purse and pulled out the gun. Even though the bedroom door was locked, she knew it would be no match for Chetti's goons. They'd kick it off the hinges if need be.

Nessa wasn't sure if Chetti had seen her last night. She still remembered Chetti looking in the direction of the door. She wasn't sure though if she'd ducked back into the shadows quick enough. Had Chetti seen her? If so, what would happen from here on out, Nessa wondered?

"The AIDS virus ain't got shit on me," Nessa could remember Chetti saying from the doorway the night Luke brought her home from the beating and kidnapping. "I've had more muthafuckas killed than the Vietnam War."

Nessa clutched the handle of the gun tightly. She would kill that old bitch if she had to. From this point, she knew that no matter what, she had to be vigil and be on standby. Her gun had to always be in arm's reach.

Slipping could be fatal.

Sighing and dropping her head, Nessa wondered if she was getting in too deep. She wondered if maybe she was getting a little over her head. Nessa wondered if she should just get out now…leave Luke behind and abandon her mother's plans. A moment later, she convinced herself that the possible rewards were worth it. If she stayed focused, she could run the family. She could have it all. It was because of that realization that she refused to walk away. She'd come too far.

A text came through.

Grabbing her phone, Nessa saw the text was from Brandon. He asked her if she still wanted him to go with her to see her father. She returned a text telling him yes. Moments later, she hit the shower and then began to get dressed. As she did, she looked out of the window and saw Trinity sitting outside by the pool. Quickly putting on her makeup, she headed downstairs and outside. As she approached, Trinity, she wasn't quite sure what she was going to say to her. Nessa knew it wasn't a good idea at all to tell her what she'd seen. She knew it would cause something far beyond drama. But at the same time, Nessa liked Trinity. She saw Trinity as someone she could consider a friend.

"What's good, girl?" Trinity asked while lying on a towel near the Jacuzzi flipping through the latest *Juicy* Magazine and drinking a glass of tequila.

"Nothing much," Nessa answered in a soft tone. "What's up with you?"

"I just met up with Darien. He said they might've found the bastard who pulled the trigger on Gavin."

"That's good to hear," Nessa responded dryly.

Silence.

Birds chirping.

Waves rippling lightly in the pool.

Then…

"Trinity, I know you told me I shouldn't ask certain things but I have to ask you something."

"What is it? Some shit must got you shook. You all quiet and shit."

A pause.

Then…

"Trinity, how did Cedrick die?"

Trinity looked at Nessa strangely. "Why do you wanna know?" She lifted her body slightly and closed the magazine.

"It's just that I've heard so much about him."

Trinity nodded understandingly. "He was killed."

"Was there a funeral?"

Trinity opened her mouth to answer. Just as she did, Chetti stepped outside. "Trinity, come here."

Nessa turned to see Chetti standing at the door glaring at her with a wicked smirk.

"What do you want?" Trinity asked.

"Don't ask me what I want, Trick. You're in *my* damn house. Come *see* what I want."

Trinity sighed in annoyance. God, how she hated

that old woman. She hated her ass with a passion.

"And I know your ass ain't drinking none of my damn tequila. You know that shit is off limits to anyone in this house besides me!" Chetti yelled.

"Bitch," Trinity muttered under her breath. She moved at a slow pace.

"Now, Trinity. Right now. Hurry."

Shaking her head, Trinity stood up, slipped her feet into her flip flops and headed towards her mother. Reaching her, they chatted softly and headed inside. As they did, Chetti gave Nessa one last look. The look was of something Nessa wasn't quite sure of. She couldn't tell if it was just of the regular dislike Chetti had for her or if it was a glare meant to let her know that she'd seen her at the door last night. Whatever it was, Nessa just shook her head and left to meet Brandon.

Sneaking to her car fretfully once the bodyguards started to change shifts, Nessa called Luke once again. And once again, there was no answer. The call went straight to voicemail. Irritated and thinking Luke was with that white woman again, she tossed the phone back into her purse and focused on the road ahead. Twenty minutes later, she pulled up at a JW Marriot on Pennsylvania Avenue where Brandon waited outside.

"Hey, sexy," Brandon said as he slid into the passenger seat and kissed Nessa.

"Hey," she returned.

"Came up with a plan."

"For what?"

"For your father. You said you want to see him locked up, right?"

"Yeah."

"All right, well I figured something out."

"What?"

"You'll see."

Several minutes later, Nessa and Brandon were pulling into the lot of the East Potomac Park once again where Nessa was to meet her father. Climbing out of the car, the two headed down a walkway. In the approaching distance seeing her father sitting on a bench and reading a newspaper, Nessa told Brandon, "That's him right there."

The two approached Byron.

Seeing his daughter, Byron folded his paper and placed it on his lap while outstretching his arms along the back of the bench. "There's my baby girl," he said with a smile.

"Quit fucking calling me that," Nessa demanded.

Her father chuckled. "Who's your friend?"

"Don't worry about that," Brandon told him. "Nessa tells me you're harassing her."

"I wouldn't call it harassing. Harassing is such a harsh word. I would prefer to call it getting a piece of the pie. Shit, I'm her daddy. I bust the fucking nut that brought her into this world. Shouldn't I get a little recognition for that? Isn't that worth something?"

Brandon didn't answer. In his mind he called Byron all kinds of sorry muthafuckas and worthless bastards.

Byron opened the paper, then pointed to an article. "I see your boyfriend here is investing in that big ass mall they're getting ready to build out in the suburbs. That nigga's loaded so it ain't like Nessa here can't afford to cut me in on some of that action."

Nessa's eyes widened. She had no idea what Luke had planned. She was pissed at that fact that he never told her anything.

"What exactly do you want?" Brandon asked.

"I don't want handouts. I want back in the game. I was a legend out here in these fuckin' streets once. I want to be a legend again."

"Really?" Brandon smirked. Well, Luke has sent me here to let you know he's willing to help you out. Because of Nessa, he's willing to let you in on some action."

Byron smiled. His teeth were a mixture of brown and yellow; at least the few teeth he still had remaining. "What kind of action?"

"We'll be in touch," Brandon told him. "I didn't catch your name."

"Byron...Byron Kingston."

"Got it." Taking her hand, Brandon and Nessa turned and walked off.

"What kind of action?" Nessa asked curious to know herself.

"The kind that carries no less than ten years in Federal Prison."

Mr. Kingston was being set up.

Nessa smiled. "Thank you, baby." She kissed him on the cheek.

"Don't worry about it. Now, we've got to make this meeting with this L.A. crew."

The two hopped back into Nessa's car. Thirty minutes later, they were pulling up in front of a Motel 6 on Allentown Road.

"Park right there," Brandon said, pointing to a spot in between a Crown Victoria and a Toyota Camry.

Nessa did as she was told.

Looking over at the Crown Victoria, Brandon rolled down his window. The person in the Crown Victoria did the same.

"Are they in there?" Brandon asked.

"Yup," the freckled-face man in the driver's seat of the Crown Victoria answered dressed in a cheap suit. He was definitely a Fed. He looked past Brandon towards

Nessa. "Who the hell is that?"

"Nobody."

"Look, Brandon, we're already taking a chance being here talking to these muthafuckas. The last thing we need is another witness. Unlike you, I care about my damn pension."

"Just relax. She's good," Brandon assured.

Nessa smiled. She knew at that moment that Brandon trusted her. Even though he hadn't admitted to her that he was a Fed, this was all the confirmation she needed.

"That's the same thing every Fed said about a piece of pussy just before they went down on corruption charges," the freckled guy added.

"Anyway, how many are in there?"

"Just ole boy and two of his goons."

Brandon looked at the motel room door ahead of him. After pausing for a second, he told Nessa, "Ready? Let's go in."

The two exited the car.

"You hear anything you don't like, you come in," Brandon told his partner.

"I got you."

Brandon knocked on the door of the motel room.

Seconds passed.

The door opened.

A tall menacing looking Mexican man appeared with a gun in his hand. Looking scornfully at Brandon, he then looked at Nessa. "Who the fuck is this?"

"A friend," Brandon replied.

"Fuck you bring her here for?"

"Look, either you muthafuckas want to talk or you don't." Brandon was super firm.

The Mexican turned and looked at his boss man, another Mexican who looked even more menacing than him.

His name was Londo. He sat in a chair with a sawed off shotgun laying across his lap and watching the entire exchange. Another man was leaning against a nearby wall holding a gun also.

"What's up, Ese`" the goon at the door asked his boss. "Let the bitch in, too?"

Londo nodded.

Brandon and Nessa stepped inside. As soon as they did, the door was shut behind them. All sets of eyes were on their every move, except Londo's whose were surveying Nessa's curves. "This yo' bitch, homie?" he asked Brandon. "I mean y'all just friends or are you puttin' dick to that pretty black ass?"

Disrespectful son of a bitch, Nessa said to herself.

"Londo, that's not important right now. We're here to talk business," Brandon said.

"*I* decide what's important, Ese`. I decide what we talk about." His eyes once again roamed Nessa's body. "Ever had some Mexican dick in that ass, Mamacita?" Londo asked.

Brandon knew the name Ese` meant homeboy or even nigga in the Spanish world, but he still hater it for some reason.

"Fuck you," Nessa spewed.

Click-Click!!!!!

The two gunmen cocked their guns.

Nessa tensed inside but never showed any sign of fear.

Brandon tensed as well.

"Fuck you think you talkin' to, bitch?" one of the gunmen asked while aiming his gun directly at Nessa.

Nessa didn't answer. She frowned, real stern like...the same way a hard-hitting nigga in the street would.

174

Chuckling, Londo leaned back into his chair with his eyes still on Nessa. "Stand down, niggas. It's cool. It's cool. No harm taken."

The men uncocked their guns.

Both Nessa and Brandon silently let out sighs of relief.

"Are we ready to talk business?" Brandon asked.

Smirking at Nessa, Londo looked back at Brandon. "Alright, let's talk."

"Shooting up the funeral wasn't a good look. They're pissed about that shit."

"So fuckin' what. That Darien nigga had no business shooting at my folks."

"You guys killed his nephew," Brandon informed.

"Collateral damage. That's the way the game goes, Ese`. He knows that," Londo replied.

"So, what do you guys want?" Brandon inquired.

Londo smiled. "The whole pie."

"That's not going to happen. But I have a suggestion."

"What's that?"

"You already know they have the purest cocaine and Meth out on the streets, right?" Brandon asked.

Londo shook his head. "Of course. Why do you think we want in?"

"Well, how about I talk to them and see if they'll put you on with their connect?"

Londo thought about it.

"If I make that happen, will you be satisfied?" Brandon asked.

Silence.

Finally…

"Yeah, Ese` I'd be satisfied."

"I'm serious, Londo. The O.K. Corral shit would

have to stop. You go back to L.A and leave D.C. alone."

Nodding, Londo said, "You make the deal happen, we'll leave D.C. alone."

"Alright, let me talk with the family and I'll get back to you on it."

"You've got three days," Londo warned.

Brandon nodded. "Bet." Minutes later, he and Nessa were back in her car driving. "Sorry that clown disrespected you in there," he said.

"Fuck him," Nessa responded.

"Like the way you handled yourself though," he told her while leaning in close. "That shit was a turn on." Brandon then slipped his hand in between her thighs, rubbed her pussy. "Let's stop by the Westin in Georgetown and get a quick one in."

Nessa agreed. She could see the pussy was guiding him. He was a hound. And as long as she kept whipping the pussy on him, she could depend on him to handle her dirty work.

A text suddenly came through on Nessa's phone.

Brandon leaned back over to his seat happy to be getting ready to get some more of Nessa's kitty. As he did, Nessa checked her text message.

Meet me now. No more excuses. Your elementary school parking lot.

Leaning against the hood of her car underneath D.C.'s night sky, Piper watched the block carefully as she took puffs from her cigarette and exhaled the smoke from her lungs ahead of her. She wondered what in the hell was taking her daughter so long. They'd spoken over forty-five minutes ago and Nessa still hadn't showed up.

Filthy Rich BY: KENDALL BANKS

Just sitting in the parking lot of Keene Elementary school brought back memories. Those were the only memories Piper had where she'd actually been a good mother. As her mind flashed back to the days where she walked Nessa to her classroom, a car pulled into the lot at full speed and skidded to an abrupt stop.

Nessa hopped out with a somber look on her face and walked toward her mother, waving unenthusiastically.

"Well damn, you sure look happy to see me," her mother said, noticing how fancy her daughter was dressed. She looked her up and down knowing she was being well taken care of.

"Hey Ma," Nessa said, lifting her spirits slightly. She really wasn't in the mood. She released a fake grin.

"Girl, what the hell is wrong with you?" Piper fired. "I been trying to get with you for weeks. You been giving me the run around, and now you see me, and give me that half-ass wave." Piper smacked her lips loudly. "Girl, remember, I gave you life. You came outta this pussy."

Nessa hated hearing those words. They always made her feel guilty…like she owed her mother her life. "Ma, it's not like that. I've just been going through something?"

"Umm hmmn," Piper sighed loudly. "I used to walk yo' ass to this school every day when you was little," she said, pointing to the building.

Nessa pivoted on one leg and crossed her arms, allowing her mother to finish venting before she spoke. "Yeah, and you left me with Daddy, too. You remember?"

"Don't you fucking go blaming me for that shit, Nessa! You know I was planning on getting you from your father," Piper added, with tears forming in the corner of her eyes. "Take that shit back!" she screamed. "Charles tricked me, and you know that!" Her voice was now at a much higher pitch.

"Ma, do I have to hear this story again? I mean really. It won't change the past."

Despite Nessa's plea, Piper began, "No matter what, I'm going to make sure you're always taken care of," that fucka Charles Bishop told me. "You'll never have to worry about anything. I promise you that."

Those words played inside Piper's head as she mocked Luke's dead father. They'd played inside her mind over the past five years more times than she could count. She heard them in her sleep. She heard them in her dreams. She heard them during her conversations with other people. She definitely heard them when she drank. The voice still sounded just as fresh as it did so many years ago. It still sounded just as loving, just as genuine. But more importantly, just as believable.

Those words would never leave her.

As she thought back in time, she could still see Charles' face. She could still feel his touch.

"Nessa, I was there for that man and he fucked me!" she said kicking the tire to her car. "And when he was in the early stages of his hustle I was there! That nigga was just moving ounces in the street!"

"Ma, I know…"

"He had an entire fuckin' family that I knew nothing about! That nigga was juggling us both while I was building his ass an empire. He fuckin' played me!"

Nessa zoned out. She knew the rest of the story. Piper was the one who'd expressed how important it was for him to expand. She'd suggested he graduate to moving actual weight, instead of small timing. The advice paid off. He got his weight up, connected with a plug and began moving kilos in no time.

Nessa knew that Piper carried guns for Charles. She

strapped bricks around her stomach and took trips on the Greyhound across state lines for him. She even took a few cases for him. She was basically a "Ride or Die Chick". Back then, she saw it as simply doing what a woman was supposed to do for her man. She was holding him down.

"Ma, I can't understand why after all this time you can't just let it go."

"Because he fuckin' promised me," Piper screamed through clinched teeth. She'd become enraged at the thought of Nessa not understanding her plight. "He made countless promises, promises that at the time changed my life. I lost everything! Even you! And now I want my revenge!"

From the moment Charles left Piper completely to be with Chetti solely, she'd been a bitter and hateful woman. She felt her bitterness and hatred was justified though. After everything she'd done to help Charles reach the top, he left her high and dry for another bitch; it didn't matter that it was his wife. Piper never got over that.

As years passed, a yearning for vengeance consumed Piper. She felt she was owed. She wanted everything Charles had. She wanted everything he'd earned. She felt she deserved it. And even after killing him, her yearning for his wealth never died. If anything, it grew. It grew so large that she decided to get Nessa involved, sending her into Luke's life knowing she would make excellent bait.

"Nessa baby," Piper said, rushing over to Nessa. "I'm sorry for acting so irrational but every time I think about all that time I lost with you, I get mad. Look how you had to go to Child Protective Services and I wasn't there to save you, or protect you. Look how many Thanksgivings and Christmases we've missed together."

Nessa too began to get teary-eyed. Thoughts of her

young life without her mother bothered her often. She
loved her mother dearly, and even though she felt like
Piper wasn't good for her, she always wanted her in her
life for fear she'd lose her again.

"If I had only known Nessa, I swear I would've
been there." Piper wrapped her arms around Nessa as they
cried together. Years of pain, hurt, love, and mistakes all
filled them. For Nessa it felt good having her mother hug
her. It didn't matter that Piper was a crazy, vengeful, vin-
dictive type of woman. It was the woman who'd given her
birth. It was maternal love.

Releasing from their hold, Piper told her, "My past
is why I told you we're not taking no more shit off those
Bishop's. We're getting their money one way or another.
And you girl, you dragging your feet thinking that nigga,
Luke loves you. He'll do the same shit to you that Charles
did to me if you let him."

"Ma, I was just trying to get him to marry me. I fig-
ured we could get more that way. That was it," Nessa lied.
She would never tell her mother she was willing to die for
Luke not long ago. Now she felt like a complete idiot.

"Nah, we'll get more by smoking and robbing them
muthafuckas. You know where that niggas stash houses
are, right?"

"Yeah, but he doesn't keep a lot of money at those
spots. And it's too complicated. They move money like
three times a day."

"Blah, blah, blah. Doesn't matter, Nessa. Step up. I
been having Luke's ass followed, and I called him asking
about you the other day. We can find out ANYTHING we
need to know."

Nessa was completely shocked. She thought about
Luke being angry that a woman called him asking about
her.

"That was you? That was stupid! Why would you do that?"

"Because you weren't fuckin' calling me back. I wanted to show yo' ass I got connections."

Nessa sighed. She knew dealing with her mother always came with problems. She thought back to her younger years when Piper and her father fought constantly. Those thoughts made Nessa tell Piper what her father had been up to.

"Look, we've got another problem," Nessa emitted.

"And what's that?"

"Dad."

"Your sorry ass father? What about him?"

"He sent a recording of the killing of Luke's father to me at Luke's house. Our faces showed and all." Nessa paused to analyze the distraught look on Piper's face. "...He's up to no good again, Ma. We gotta do something about him."

Piper took a few minutes to process everything her daughter was saying. Her head kept shaking back and forth while she made grunting sounds. Deep down inside she despised Byron. Their eleven years together had been nothing worth remembering, just lots of pain, struggle, fussing, and torture. "Let me work on that nigga," she finally said.

"Don't kill him, Ma. Just stop him. I already have somebody else working on putting his ass in jail, so nothing crazy."

"Look Nessa, I got this. I'll handle your father. He hasn't seen my face in thirteen years, but it's time he caught my wrath once more. And you..." she paused and pointed her finger, "...no more bullshitting with the Bishops. Get back to that house and devise a plan that doesn't involve marrying the enemy. Those fuckas stole our lives. Find out where they keep the major money and I'll decide how we gon' kill all of them."

Nessa didn't like that plan at all. She had plans of her own that she couldn't share with her mother just yet. After a few more hugs, Nessa hopped back in her ride, waving goodbye, wondering if she and Piper would ever have that mother-daughter relationship she yearned for.

Darien climbed out of his Aston Martin, walked up the walkway to the condo and rang the doorbell. Seconds later, the door opened. Luke stood there dressed in plain clothing; a black Versace t-shirt and black jeans, something he rarely wore. He invited Darien inside.

"Want a drink?" he asked.

"Nahhh," Darien said smugly. "So what'd you want to talk about?"

The two sat in the spacious living room.

"Have you given any thought whatsoever to getting out of the game?" Luke asked his brother as he leaned back into the cushions of the couch and crossed his legs.

"Nope."

"Darien, how long do you think we can keep dodging bullets and Fed time out here?"

Sighing, Darien told him, "Look, if that's what you called me over here for, you're wastin' your time and breath."

"Look bro, I've got something that will change your life forever."

"I like my life…but what is it?"

"A deal that could put you in a position to get out the streets."

Darien sighed gain.

"A deal that could make you millions legitimately,"

Luke continued. "It wouldn't require any hard work. Just an investment."

"What is it?"

"I'm investing in that mall they're getting ready to build on the other side of town."

"The one they're sayin' is gonna be the biggest one in the state of Maryland?" Darien questioned.

"Yeah, I'm investing millions into it. The payoff is going to be huge."

"So what does that shit have to do with me?"

"I want you to come in on half my end; I need twenty-five million from your stocks and bonds."

Darien didn't say anything a first. Then came a chuckle. "Nigga, you crazy."

"Darien, that mall is going to be a goldmine. It's going to bring us millions of dollars per year. All we'll have to do is sit back and collect payment."

"And what about the money in the streets?"

"What about it? I told you I'm leaving that shit alone."

Darien shook his head. "Sorry, bruh, but I'm still not willin' to leave behind what we worked fo', especially right now. Muthafuckas thinkin' we soft right now. Besides, I'm only thirty years old. It's too damn early for me to retire."

"Darien, hear me out."

"My mind is made up, Luke. I'm stayin' in the game."

Just then, Luke's co-investor, Pamela Benson appeared from a backroom dressed in one of Luke's button down shirts. It was clear she wore no panties underneath. "Oh, I'm sorry, Luke," she said seeing Darien. "I didn't know we had company."

"You're okay?" Luke told her.

"We?" Darien mocked then gazed at his brother.

"I'm going to take a shower. Where are the new towels I bought?" she asked, licking her lips seductively in Luke's direction.

"They're in the top drawer of the dresser."

"Okay sexy," she said after blowing a few seductive kisses.

She disappeared.

Darien looked at his brother and shook his head. "See, that's your damn problem right there."

"What?"

"*That*, nigga," Darien said, pointing to where Pamela had just been standing. "Pussy."

"What are you talking about?"

"First, you move Nessa's ass into our house. Now, you over here shacked up wit' a white bitch who's in desperate need of some ass injections." Darien shook his head once again. "See, that's why I only bang black chicks. They got ass for days."

"Darien, let me handle my relationship issues. I just need you to help me financially on this deal. I can't do it without you, bro."

"Bro my ass, you doin' some crazy shit all of a sudden. No wonder you're talkin' 'bout gettin' out the game. What, you gon' become a Jehovah's Witness next? You gon' be out here goin' from door to door sellin' *Watch Towers* and shit? Or are you gonna be one of them muthafuckas standin' at the stoplight in a bowtie and suit sellin' *Final Calls* and bean pies?"

Luke sighed. "You're tripping."

"Oh, *I'm* the one who's trippin'?"

"Yes."

Darien stood and headed for the kitchen. He grabbed a banana off of the counter and peeled off the covering. "You startin' to lose sight of how you was raised. Ma may not be perfect, but she's taught us a whole lot. One of the most important things she's taught us evidently you've forgot."

"Oh yeah? And what's that?"

Luke's expression suddenly turned into a blatant frown. He was glad he'd heard the shower water start.

"She taught us that pussy will get your ass killed."

Luke rushed over to Darien, his insides boiling. His voice began to tremble as he spoke closely in his brother's face. "Our mother doesn't deserve an award for the way she raised us. She needs to be locked up or gunned down instead!"

Darien's eyes lit up as he took a step back, and bit off a large piece of the banana.

"Your mother and father have been and always will be animals!" he shouted.

Luke's face was now flushed. It was clear his emotions had gotten the best of him. He turned several times to make sure the sounds of water flowing from the shower was still happening. What he needed to say to Darien couldn't be heard by anyone but a Bishop.

"They drugged and forced me to sleep with my own sister, for God's sake! Isn't that enough to let you know they were never responsible parents." At that moment, Luke flashed back to hearing his father say, '*Just keeping the bloodline pure*' while he watched Luke fuck his sister.

The thought and memory of that night infuriated Luke, and made him want to vomit. Strangely, none it fazed Darien.

"Luke, what's done is done. Let that shit go, bruh. I'm just worried about gettin' this money.

"So, you're okay with this shit!"

He shrugged his shoulders.

Suddenly, Luke gazed into his brother's eyes, and spoke softer, with total resentment. "Gavin was born with muscular dystrophy because of incest. There are cousins of ours who are slow, almost fuckin' retarded because of the Bishop family incest. And you're telling me it's not that bad."

"Nigga, look. Fuck all that. We got that one bitch that live down south with that crooked ass face," Darien said, while throwing his peeling in the trash, and walking toward the door. "That bitch's momma and daddy ugly as fuck, so we can't really blame that on incest. Besides, do your research bruh, not all children born from two relatives come out fucked up. That's a myth." Darien grabbed at his crotch. "And here I was thinkin' you was the smart one."

Luke thought about Darien's last comment. He was partially correct. The percentages of children born from incest with disabilities was low, but Luke didn't care. It was wrong. And he hated his parents for forcing him to be involved, along with his mother's other secrets.

Darien had grabbed the knob to the front door by the time Luke walked in his direction.

"I wasn't finished," Luke emitted.

"As far as I'm concerned, this is over. I got freaks waitin' on me. Ones with fat asses."

Darien closed the door and left.

Filthy Rich BY: KENDALL BANKS

Chapter 17

Luke hadn't quite slept the night before. So many things were on his mind. He had so many plans and so many good intentions but so much was standing in between himself and a much bigger future than his present; his family specifically. They were his Achilles heel. He realized now that there was no way around the decision he was going to have to make.

Luke would have to pull away by any means necessary.

Darien had it wrong about Luke being influenced these days by pussy. Pamela was more than just pussy for Luke. She was more than just a conquest. Pamela's family were billionaires. They owned multimillion dollar businesses and franchises on several different continents. They had connections in politics, law enforcement, on Wall Street, entertainment and so many other facets of life. They were a conglomerate, and Luke wanted a piece of it.

When Pamela began to take an interest in Luke, he was still honestly in love with Nessa. But quickly the business side of him took over. He realized Pamela had much more to offer. With her by his side, there was no way he could fail at taking his family to the highest levels of legitimate corporate success, especially if he and Pamela eventually got married; that was partially why he'd decided over the last few days to move Pamela in with him.

Luke was still contemplating on how to keep Nessa at the house with Chetti. Nessa had been cool while it lasted but she was a hood rat. She knew nothing about politics. She knew nothing about high-stakes investing. She wouldn't know how to move in a ballroom of important people, specifically the wives of powerful and successful men. She'd be lost. Luke knew that. Pamela was obviously the better choice.

The only choice.

Besides the Pamela and Nessa situation, Luke's conscience had also been tormenting him. He thought about his brother Cedrick more times the night before than he had over the entire past several years. He realized his brother was completely right for wanting to take the family out the streets. Luke just wished he had realized it back then. He wished he would've had the heart to stand up for his brother.

Luke couldn't change the past, he now came to grips with. But he could surely build the future. The first thing he was going to begin with was Cedrick. Cedrick had been a prisoner in that damn room long enough.

Luke was dressed and in his car within minutes. While driving, he knew taking Cedrick out of that house was going to be met with conflict. He knew his mother would claw, scratch and kick to keep that horrible secret protected. That was why he chose to bring a gun; his nine millimeter with him. If he had to kill to free his brother, so be it.

Luke's thoughts were diverted when his cell phone rang.

Sighing, not really interested in talking to Nessa, Luke answered anyway. "Yeah," he said while placing the phone to his ear.

"Why haven't you been answering your phone?" Nessa asked.

"Business."

"And you couldn't step away from business long enough to answer my damn calls or my texts?"

"Nessa, I was busy. That's the end of it."

"No, it's not the fucking end of it, Luke. Is there another bitch?"

"Nessa, quit acting like a child."

"Just answer the question, Luke!"

Luke simply sighed. He knew he'd have to tell Nessa that they needed some space; space for him to secretly build his relationship with Pamela. He'd also have to tell her that plans had changed, and that she wasn't moving with him to the condo. *No better time than now*, he thought.

"I'm sick of this shit, Luke. You don't fuck me like you used to. You won't give me a child. You don't spend any time with me. And you don't want to talk about marriage. What the hell?"

"Shit's complicated. I just need some space to get business done for a while."

"And what the fuck is that supposed to mean?"

"It means I want you to stay at the house with my mother for a while, just until I get things settled. It's too dangerous for you to stay with me anymore."

"You're some bullshit, Luke!"

"Nessa, you're reading too much into things."

"No, I'm not. I'm in this damn house all day every day by myself surrounded by fucking secrets. No one wants to talk to me about anything. No one wants to tell me anything. Shit, you're even lying to me about what's in that damn room your mother keeps locked."

The final sentence of Nessa's rant drew Luke's attention completely. "You said what about that room?"

Nessa quieted.

"Nessa, what did you say about that room?" he asked again more sternly.

"I said, I know you're lying to me about what's in that room that your mother keeps locked. I don't feel safe here, Luke!"

"Nessa, let me tell you something. The secrets of that house, including whatever's in that room, are none of your fucking concern. Those secrets were there *before* you and they will be there *after* you. Leave it alone. Do you understand?"

She didn't answer.

"Do you fucking understand?" he roared.

"Yeah," she answered.

"I'm on my way home. Stay put."

He ended the call.

The young lady's name was Raquel. Her frame was thick. Her ass was well rounded and fat. Her breasts were full. Her hair was long. Her face was pretty. But most importantly…She was eighteen.

The lights of the den were dim as Chetti poured a glass of tequila for her first cousin's beautiful daughter. Smiling, Chetti made like a gracious host as she showed her niece she was happy to see her after so many years. In reality though, it was simply an act.

"How's your mother?" Chetti asked, not really interested but pretending like she was as she handed Raquel the glass.

"She's good," Raquel answered. "Umm, Chetti, you know I'm not old enough to drink yet, right?"

Chetti frowned. "Girl, stop all that damn whining and drink up. Age ain't nothing but a number around here. Besides, if I told you some of the stories about what your hoe-ass mother did at your age, you would be amazed."

"But…" Raquel tried to say.

"But nothing. You better not waste my good tequila."

Raquel quickly sipped from the glass.

"Now, how's your brother?"

"He's good.

"Great." Chetti sat down at the head of the table as usual. "So, what are you planning on doing now that you're out of high school?"

"College."

"Oh, what college are you planning on attending?"

"I've got several offers. I'm thinking about Stanford."

Nodding with approval, Chetti said, "Great choice. That's an excellent college."

"I still need a letter of recommendation though."

"Why didn't you tell me? I have important friends in high places who can supply you with several letters of recommendation."

Raquel's face brightened. "Are you serious?"

"Of course. You're like a niece to me. Whatever I can do to get you on a successful path, I'm all for it."

"Thank you, Chetti."

"Don't worry about it."

The two began to talk more.

Time passed.

Raquel began to grow intoxicated. It wasn't a normal intoxication though. It felt strange, stranger than any other she'd ever felt. It had also come on much quicker than any other she'd experienced. She tried to fight it off as she and Chetti talked. But no matter how hard she fought, it grew more and more intense. Her words became slurred. Little did Raquel know, Chetti had slipped more than tequila into her glass. Rohypnol, better known as a roofie could be felt within thirty minutes of being drugged and could last for several hours, so it was definitely Chetti's weapon of choice.

Seeing how woozy Raquel grew, Chetti began to maneuver the conversation from worldly topics to more intimate ones. "Do you have a boyfriend?" she asked.

"No."

"Why not?"

"I just want to concentrate on school."

"But a girl as beautiful as you has to make time for fun. Surely you have at least a little bit of side dick, of course."

Raquel giggled. "Not really. Like I said, I'm completely focused on school."

The room began to spin for Raquel. Her head began to ache. She looked at the glass of tequila strangely.

"You okay?" Chetti asked, knowing she wasn't.

"What kind of concoction is this?"

Ignoring her baby cousin's question, Chetti stood and made her way along the table toward her. Coming up behind her, she placed her hands on her shoulders and began to massage them. She then placed her lips close to Raquel's ear and whispered, "The world can be yours, baby. I can give you much more than even Stanford College can give you. I can give you everything you've ever dreamed of, everything you've ever wanted."

Raquel's head began to spin. The mixture of the

wine's effects and Chetti's massage soothed her.

"I can give you fortunes, shopping sprees, vacations in the islands," Chetti continued. "You'd never have to work. You'd never have to lift a finger."

Chetti's hands began to make their way from Raquel's shoulders to her shirt. They then slowly reached inside and began to caress her breasts.

Raquel wanted to stop what was happening. At least a part of her did but the tequila's hold on her wouldn't allow her to. Another part of her though was enjoying Chetti's touch and caresses. It all felt divine but so wrong all at the same time.

"You can have it all, Raquel," Chetti whispered. Her hands were now inside Raquel's bra. Her fingers were now squeezing her hardening nipples. "Don't you want that, baby?"

Raquel closed her eyes and leaned back into her older cousin. She couldn't help herself.

"Don't you, baby?" Chetti asked again, this time with her hands now making their way down to Raquel's skirt. "Don't you want that, princess?"

Chetti slipped her hands underneath Raquel's skirt and into her panties. She then inserted two fingers inside her wetness. Raquel moaned as she opened her thighs to give her auntie better access.

"You're eighteen now, Raquel. You can make your own decisions. You can do what you want now. No one can stop you."

Chetti's whispering words hypnotized Raquel while the feel of her fingers working in and out of her made her kitty leak.

"Do you want the world?"

"Yessssss," Raquel moaned.

Rubbing Raquel's clit, Chetti asked, "Do you *really*

want it?"

"Yesssssssssss," Raquel moaned louder totally under Chetti's spell.

Smiling and satisfied, Chetti took her fingers out of her niece's pussy and backed away. She then headed to the door and opened it. Leaning against the wall beside the door was Darien. Still smiling, she approached him, kissed him on the lips and said sinisterly, "She's ready, sweetheart. Go put a baby in that bitch."

Darien nodded and headed into the den closing the door.

Chetti placed her back against the door, proud of what she'd done. Leaning her head back and wrapping her arms around herself, she closed her eyes and listened. Moments later, she could hear Raquel moaning as Darien stroked himself into her. The sound made Chetti smile even bigger than before. With her eyes still closed, she whispered, "That's right, baby. Keep the bloodline pure."

The clicking of heels sounded.

Moments later, Chetti opened her eyes to see Nessa looking at her. Her smile disappeared. A look of spite replaced it. "What the fuck do you want?"

"Where's Trinity?" Nessa asked.

Chetti chuckled. "Somewhere her ungrateful ass should've been a long time ago."

"What does that mean?"

Leaving Nessa standing there, Chetti didn't answer. She simply walked off while laughing loudly. The further away from Nessa she disappeared, the louder her laughs grew.

Chapter 18

Luke's car zoomed up to the bottom of the mansion's steps. He wondered why there wasn't any security on post near the front gates. Turning off the engine, he sat still for a moment. Pressing his hands into his temples, he just shook his head repeatedly. Pulling out the gun, he studied it, and silently began to ask himself if the decision he was making was the correct one. Was this really what he wanted? And was he really willing to kill his mother and brother if it came down to it? He closed his eyes and pondered over it all. Several moments later, he opened them. He had his answer.

This was what he wanted.

Dressed casually, in a pair of Hugo Boss, jeans he slid out of the car and closed its door. Making his way around the hood, he stuffed the gun underneath his shirt and jogged up the steps. Reaching the door, he opened it and walked into the foyer to find the house quiet.

Again, no security.

Where was everyone?

Wasting no time, he headed directly to the den to grab some important papers he knew he would need.

196

Reaching the den, he opened the door and was startled to find both Darien and Raquel fucking missionary style on top of the table.

"What the fuck!" Luke yelled.

"Damn, nigga, don't you knock?" Darien asked naked.

If there were any lingering doubts in Luke's head about leaving this life and the mansion behind, the sight of his brother fucking their own cousin did away with all of them.

A silence proceeded.

Luke gave his brother a look he usually only gave to people whom he held heavy contempt for. Darien recognized it.

That repulsed look.

Darien could tell by his gaze that something had changed between him and his brother. Some sort of line had been crossed. He didn't care though. Now out of spite, while continuing to stare across the den into Luke's eyes, he began to stroke deeply inside Raquel once again. A moment later, while still looking into his brother's eyes, he began to pound Raquel harder and harder. A sick smile began to come across his face.

"Oh God!" Raquel screamed in pleasure.

Shaking his head and realizing he and his brother were done, Luke slammed the door and headed up the stairs. "Nessa!" he called as he reached their bedroom.

There was no answer.

Nessa was nowhere in sight.

Refusing to waste time looking for her, Luke made his way to Cedrick's room pulling out the key he'd been holding onto for years. He unlocked the door and opened it. To his surprise though, Cedrick wasn't in there. He quickly began to search the room and bathroom but still couldn't find Cedrick. Wondering what was going on, he paused for a moment. He then charged out of the room yelling for his mother. Not receiving an answer, he continued calling as he made his way down the grand staircase. As he reached the bottom, suddenly…

BOOM!!!!!

The front door flew open. A split second later…

"Get your ass down on the floor!"

"Get down now!"

Dozens of Federal and ATF agents all dressed in black and in ski masks came rushing into the grand foyer with guns pointed. They immediately scattered like ants. Infrared lasers pointed everywhere, several directly at Luke.

"Get the fuck down, muthafucka, before we blow your head off!"

Luke had no choice but to do as he was told. He lay down on his belly with his arms stretched outward. A moment later, an agent pounced on him, took his gun from underneath his shirt and placed him in hand cuffs.

The agents began to make their way throughout the house. Lying on his stomach, Luke watched as several agents approached the den. He then watched as they kicked the door open. Seconds later, he watched them bring both Darien and Raquel out naked and in handcuffs.

"Fuck you, muthafuckas!" Darien yelled defiantly at the agents as he was forced towards where Luke was laying. He spit globs of saliva at every agent who made the mistake of getting to close. "Fuck you bitches!"

"Get the fuck off me!" Chetti screamed as an agent began to escort her down the stairs handcuffed from wherever she'd been. "You have no right to be in my damn house. Where's your warrant?"

"Miss, you are under arrest. You…" an agent attempted to say.

"Fuck you," she spat. "Do you know who I am?" Chetti quickly interrupted.

Ignoring her, the agent continued reading her rights. He then forced her to lie down directly next to Luke.

"I want my damn lawyer!" Chetti continued screaming. "I will own this damn city!"

Luke shook his head when saw Nessa being dragged in from the back of the house. She was handcuffed and forced to lie down beside Raquel.

As Chetti and Darien yelled and cursed at the agents from the floor, Luke focused on the top of the staircase. He was expecting to see Cedrick brought down at any moment. But as he watched, he only saw agents.

Moments later, Brandon and several other Feds walked into the house. As they did, Brandon glanced at his family sprawled out on the floor, a family his fellow agents didn't know he was related to. Both Chetti and Darien gave him a glare that silently asked, "Son of a bitch, why didn't you let us know we were going to get hit?" Brandon didn't return their stares though. Instead, he walked over to Luke and started at him.

"We finally got your ass," Brandon said.

"Yeah, we finally got 'em," another agent agreed.

"How does it feel to know that you're going away for a long ass time?" Brandon looked back at his fellow agents. "Hey, which one of you wants the Bentley? I think he just purchased that one."

All the agents laughed.

Luke knew Brandon was just playing the role of asshole in order to throw things off, but he was taking things too far. When he gave a "that's enough" look, Brandon finally walked into another room.

Luke continued to watch the stairs. Still no Cedrick.

Not even Trinity.

"Clear!" an agent yelled moments later. "There's no one else here!"

Perplexed, Luke looked over at his mother and asked, "Where's Cedrick?"

She didn't answer.

"Mother, where is Cedrick?"

Still no answer.

"Mother, answer me. Where is he?"

Chetti just continued to wallow in her words and filthy outburst. She acted as if she didn't hear her son speaking to her.

"Where's Trinity, Mother?"

Finally, Chetti gave a response. It wasn't verbal though. It was a smirk.

Knowing that smirk meant something terrible, Luke asked louder than before, "Mother, what the fuck did you do to Trinity and Cedrick?"

Her smirk became a smile.

Even though, Luke could hear agents nearby talking about the cash they'd found in the basement, and multiple guns and weaponry, Luke's heart remained focused on his siblings. She'd hurt them all far too many times.

"You evil bitch, where's my brother and sister!" he yelled. "Where the fuck are they?"

A heavy-set agent with scraggily hair grabbed Luke and snatched him to his feet. He then began to escort him outside. As he did, Luke fought viciously in his cuffs while screaming at his mother, "Where's Trinity and Cedrick? Bitch, where's my family? What have you done!"

As her son was dragged out of the mansion kicking and screaming, Chetti just continued to smile knowing she knew something he didn't.

Filthy Rich BY: KENDALL BANKS

* * *

Piper watched as her television played in the living room of her small apartment. On its screen was D.C.'s latest drug bust. Camera's rolled as several people were escorted out of a huge home near the lake, and placed each in individual unmarked cars. Of all the people brought out though, one person in particular caught the woman's attention...

Nessa.

Piper leaned forward on her couch and watched as Nessa was escorted to a car while the newscaster said the family was suspected in numerous crimes, including drug trafficking, conspiracy, gun running and all types of other heavy charges. She shook her head and leaned back into the couch while developing a stressful look on her face.

"Damn it," she said in frustration. "This wasn't part of the plan, Nessa."

This latest episode hadn't been foreseen. Growing angry and worried that the plan would fall to pieces, Piper stood and then began to pace the floor. Growing enraged, she grabbed a lamp and threw it through the screen of the television. "Goddamn it, Nessa!" she screamed. "I told you to murk those muthafuckas a long time ago!"

Piper began to pace again as the television smoked. Finally, she realized there was nothing she could do. What was done was done. She sighed as she realized she could only do one thing...

Hope her daughter didn't mention her name. She'd taught her the code of the streets. She'd now see how Nessa was built.

Chapter 19

Escorted by a guard, Luke walked by several booths, each equipped with a phone, glass window, and steel chair. As he walked, he was dressed in a blue county issued jumpsuit and rubber flip flops. Reaching a booth at the far end of the hall, he entered and sat down on the steel chair. On the other side of the booth's bullet proof glass was Eric Thomas, Luke's personal business attorney. Sitting beside him was another man. Grabbing the phone from the cradle and placing it to his ear, Luke asked Eric, "Is this him?"

"Yes," Eric answered. "This is Trevor Staley."

Luke and his family had now been in jail for several days. They'd just been arraigned and told of their charges the previous day. Each charge was beyond serious. Along with being charged under the RICO Law, they were being charged with running a criminal enterprise, conspiracy, the illegal distribution of drugs and guns across state lines, racketeering and so much more. After the arraignment, Luke got directly on the phone, called Eric and told him to get the best criminal attorney he knew.

"Have you been updated on my charges?" Luke

asked Trevor.

"Yes," Trevor answered. "All very serious."

"Well, I don't care about how serious. I just need you to get me off."

"I'll do my best."

"Your best isn't good enough. I need you to get me off, *period*."

Trevor nodded.

"Did you pay my bail?" Luke asked Eric.

Everyone's bail, besides Nessa and Raquel, was each set at a half a million dollars. The two girls are set a ten grand each."

"Well, did you pay it?" Luke asked.

Eric developed an uneasy expression on his face. "Luke, your accounts have been frozen."

Luke's eyes bulged. "What?"

"All your accounts have been frozen by the Feds. I can't get any money out. And all the cash in the house was seized."

"Damn it!" Luke yelled. "Are you serious? That was a lot of fucking money!"

"Do you have any accounts I don't know about?" Eric asked.

"No." Luke dropped his head.

Silence.

"Don't worry, man, we're going to make this work."

Luke looked back up toward the glass. He had a stressful look on his face. He had another idea, but he would have to handle it a little bit later. He looked at Trevor. "Have you ever taken a case like this one before?"

"Several."

"Did you win them?"

"Six out of eight. I'm not quite sure of all the specifics of your case. I've got to go over all the paperwork. Once I see everything, I can give you a clearer answer about everything. But, Mr. Bishop, before we go further, I have to tell you my retainer fee is fifty thousand dollars."

"You'll get your money. Don't worry about that."

"Okay, I'll also have to get with the attorneys of your co-defendants and…"

"Hell no!" Luke roared. "I want my case separated from them."

"But…"

"In fact, I want immunity," Luke added.

"Mr. Bishop, the only way you can get that is if you turn on your family," Trevor explained.

"I'm fully aware of that. Get with the prosecutor and tell them I want to testify *against* my mother and brother."

Both attorneys looked at each other perplexed and then back at Luke.

"I'm serious," Luke continued. "I'm testifying against them. They were the ones running this shit, not me."

"Alright, if this is what you want," Trevor responded. He was surprised but knew in these cases, the first person to cut a deal was usually the one who would beat the case in the end. "I'll get the ball rolling."

This was it for Luke. He was breaking away from his family for good; the sick ways, the corruption, the control, everything. His mother had killed both Trinity and Cedrick. He knew it. He felt it. Even without seeing the bodies for himself, he knew exactly what that look on his mother's face expressed back at the mansion during the raid. She'd done something horrible. Luke wasn't going to let her get away with it. He was going to tell everything, including the imprisonment of his brother, Cedrick.

After another fifteen minutes of conversing about the case, Luke was escorted back to his pod. As soon as he was inside, among the laughter and yelling of all the other inmates, he headed to the CO's desk. The CO knew exactly who Luke was. He knew his power. He knew his reputation. It was because of those reasons that he slipped Luke a cellphone without anyone noticing. Luke then headed back to his cell, shut the door and made a call.

Sitting alone in a small dimly lit room in the Montgomery County Jail, Brandon listened as Luke carried on a conversation with his attorneys. Although it was illegal to listen in on conversations between attorney and client, he used his authority as a Fed to make it happen by placing a small listening device in the cellphone Luke was given by the guard. Luke might've thought he was top dog in jail, but nothing outweighed Brandon's status; especially since he'd paid the guard a nice payment to offer Luke the phone in the first place. As soon as the conversation was over, Brandon leaned back into his chair thinking about everything he'd just overheard.

Brandon would've never imagined in a million years that Luke would roll on his own family. He began to grow nervous. If Luke would turn on his own mother and brother, would he turn on Brandon? The possibility had Brandon on edge.

Brandon's cell phone rang. Pulling it from the inner pocket of his suit jacket, he saw a number on the screen he didn't recognize. He answered. "Yeah?"

"Why the *fuck* didn't you let us know we were going to get hit?" Luke's voice asked furiously.

Brandon's body tensed. He knew it was rare for

Luke to curse let alone speak in such a vicious tone. "Luke, I had no idea."

"You're a fucking Federal Agent, aren't you? How the fuck could you not know?"

"I'm not in on every investigation, Luke. This one I had no idea about. I didn't even know it was you we were coming to hit until we got close to your street. They were keeping this one top secret to avoid any leaks. There must be a rat."

"Then they may know about you."

"I doubt it. If they did, I'd be in cuffs right now," Brandon whispered.

"Brandon, you'd better not be fuckin' lying to me. Cousin or no cousin, if I find out that you were in on this bust, you're a dead man. You understand?"

"Luke, I wouldn't do that. Loyalty is everything."

"I said, do you fucking understand?!" Luke roared.

"Yeah, I understand, Luke."

"I'm gonna need you to get Nessa out of here ASAP." Her bail was only ten thousand since she was only an accessory.

"What about Raquel?" Brandon asked.

"I'll deal with that later. Right now, I need Nessa out immediately."

"Will do." Brandon replied. Where are you calling from?"

"Don't worry about it. The call isn't being monitored. Get Nessa out today, you hear me?"

"I hear you, loud and clear," Brandon told him.

"Today, Brandon. Not tomorrow. Not the day after. Get her out *today*."

"Okay, I got you. Call back in exactly fifteen minutes."

The two ended their call.

Nessa threw up in the toilet of her cell once again. For the past several days, she'd been unable to keep anything down. At first she thought it was the jail's food. But quickly realized she was throwing up even when she hadn't eaten. She couldn't understand why at first. It was getting to the point where she was sick constantly. Fortunately for her, a correctional officer had taken her to the infirmary where Nessa was given several tests and told that she was pregnant.

Nessa now sat in her cell crying profusely wondering how she ended up in jail. As thoughts filled her head an unlikely request was being made. "Ms. Kingston, you've got a visitor," a voice said over the loud speaker of her cell.

Nessa flushed the toilet, brushed her teeth and headed out of her cell anxious to see who had come to help her. Several minutes later, she found herself being escorted to a small room a few feet away from the guard's station. At the opening of its door, she saw Brandon sitting in a chair on the opposite side of a small table.

"I got her from here," Brandon told the escorting guard.

Moments later, the guard left the room and closed the door behind him.

Nessa immediately rushed into Brandon's arms.

"How are you?" he asked when they released each other. Brandon could tell she looked stressed. "You okay?"

"Yeah, I'm good," she told him. "Sick as shit, but I'm surviving." She wanted so badly to share the news about her pregnancy, but of course she couldn't. After all, she wasn't sure if her unborn child was Luke's or Brandon's.

The moment Brandon saw a tear drop, he wiped her face with his thumb. Sincerely, he spoke, "I'm going to get you out of here."

Her eyes widened. "When?"

"Today."

"Thank you. I can't take too much more of this place. It stinks. The food is horrible and I can't take it anymore. Anyway, have you guys found Cedrick?" Nessa wanted to ask that question for the past several days.

"Cedrick?" Brandon asked.

"Yeah."

"Nessa, Cedrick's dead."

"No, he's not."

"Nessa, he is. He was murdered."

"Brandon, that's why Luke was going off on his mother before y'all drug him out the house. Cedrick isn't dead."

"How do you know?"

"I saw him."

Brandon looked at her suspiciously.

"Brandon, I'm not going crazy. I know what I saw. Cedrick's not dead. I saw him with my own two eyes. Not only did I see him, but his crazy ass mother was having sex with him."

Brandon was in total disbelief. He walked away from Nessa and began pacing the floor.

"I know it sounds crazy, but it's true. And what about Trinity. Have y'all found her?"

"Not that I know of. I'm not in on the exact details of this investigation."

"I think Chetti did something to her," Nessa fired with way too much emotion. She kept fidgeting and speaking rapidly.

"Why would you think that?"

"I'm not sure but Chetti may have seen me the night I caught her in Cedrick's room with him. I think she may have killed Trinity because she thought I told her what I saw."

His cell rang. Without answering, he offered it to Nessa. "Answer; it's for you."

Nessa eyebrows crinkled. "For me? Who is it?" She was nervous and curious all at the same time.

"Just answer it."

Hesitantly, Nessa took the phone. Placing it to her ear, she said, "Hello?"

"Hey, baby," Luke said.

"Luke?" Nessa nearly screamed with surprise. "Are you okay?"

"I'm good. What about you?"

"I'm making it."

"Good, you know I love you, right?"

"Of course."

Brandon was next to her leaning against the table. The volume of the phone was loud enough for him to hear. He pursed his lips to the side when he heard Luke's question.

"Do you love me, Nessa?"

"You know I do."

"Have you spoken to anyone? Have the Feds or detectives questioned you about anything?"

"Yeah, but I know the drill, Luke. I was raised to be a soldier. I told them I didn't know anything."

"Are you sure?"

"Yes, damn, Luke. You should know by now that you can trust me."

"I know, baby. I understand. I get it. But listen carefully."

Nessa did as she was told.

"Brandon's going to get you out today. I have some money stashed; a million to be exact."

Nessa's eyebrows rose.

"The first thing I need you to do is pay my attorney. Once you've done that, I'm gonna need you to get with my connect, cop five bricks, and flip 'em. I'm going to need to make some money fast. Brandon will help you out. You hear me, Nessa."

"Yeah, I'm listening."

"You remember when I took you with me to meet Chavez?"

Nessa smiled at the thought. He was a sexy, wealthy man who controlled most of the Columbian drug trade.

"Well, Brandon knows how to get in touch with him. Once you get with Chavez, Brandon will put you in touch with the people who'll help you flip the work. As soon as you've made five hundred thousand, get me out of here. You understand."

"I got you."

"This is serious, Nessa. I need you to make this happen."

"Luke, I got you. I was bred for this."

He then told her where the money was stashed. Afterwards, once again, he told her he loved her.

"I love you, too, Luke."

"Alright, let me speak to Brandon."

She gave Brandon the phone.

The two men conversed for several moments then ended their call.

Stuffing the phone back into his pocket, Brandon shook his head in disgust and said, "Rat muthafucka."

"What are you talking about?" Nessa asked.

"He's planning on turning State's evidence on his own family."

Nessa was completely shocked. "Are you serious? How do you know?"

"I was listening in on his conversation with his attorney earlier. He wants to cut a deal. He's going to give Chetti and Darien to the Feds on a silver platter."

"Are you serious?"

"Hell fuckin' yeah, I'm serious. And that means if he's going to tell on them, he'll tell on me. That snake ass son of a bitch. He's even lying to you."

"About what?"

"All that bullshit talk about loving you. He doesn't love you. He's just saying that to get you to do what he wants. When he gets out, he's going to hook up with that white bitch."

Pressing the center button on his iPhone, Brandon pulled up a photo and showed it to Nessa. It was a photo of the same white woman he had shown her a photo of before.

"That's her on a visit here to see Luke yesterday," Brandon informed. "There's more."

Nessa swiped her finger across the touch screen to see another picture of the white woman. Her heart sunk. Hurt filled her veins.

"That's a picture of her coming to see him again today."

With the swiping of her finger, Nessa saw at least four pictures in all; Even a few of Pamela parked in front of Luke's new condo.

"She's been here every visiting day, Nessa. Her name's Pamela."

Nessa's blood boiled.

"He doesn't care about you. Like I said, he just wants you to get him what he needs. Once that's done, he's going to drop you like yesterday's garbage. He's also planning on moving Pamela into the new condo with him. Shit, he may even kill you if he knows you know about Cedrick. That nigga is foul."

Nessa leaned against the table and slipped into deep thought. *That muthufucka!* Although angry, she knew she couldn't quite be mad. Just like when she'd first heard about Pamela while back at the hotel rendezvous with Brandon, she and Luke were merely playing each other. They were both deceiving each other. It had never been more clearer than it was right now.

**You hooked up with Luke to do a job…
Get it done!!!!!**

The final text Nessa received from her mother came to mind. It etched itself into her brain.

Taking Nessa's face into his hands, Brandon looked into her eyes. "The world can be yours, Nessa. All yours. You and I can take that stash of Luke's and build our own empire. In the process, I'll see to it that he never ever gets out of jail."

Nessa smirked knowing that she was already ahead of Brandon. She was already planning inside her head to carve her own path in the game compliments of Luke's money.

"I'm in. Just me and you," she told Brandon, kissing him on the lips.

Brandon smiled widely. "And that thing with your father is being handled. My boys have already met with him once. He'll be good as caught and in an orange jump-suit in a couple weeks."

Nessa buried her head into Brandon's chest, loving that her plan was working.

Dear Diary

Shit has spiraled out of control. My plan to seek revenge on the Bishop Family is all fucked up. That damn daughter of mine has ruined everything…all in the name of love. I told that bitch, Nessa years ago that niggas ain't shit…they all need to be played. That's why I'm headed to fuck the shit out of Brandon again just to get what I want. At least that nigga came through and got them muthafuckas locked up. I'm about to show them niggas who Piper really is.

Chapter 20

The bedsprings seemed to squeak louder and louder as Piper welcomed Brandon deeply inside her. As he stroked in a constant and unwavering rhythm, she dug her nails into the flesh of his back. Piper held on tightly not wanting him to ease up from the pleasure he was inflicting.

"Fuck me, Brandon," she moaned into his ear.

"Awwwww, shit!" Brandon moaned in pleasure at the warmth of her insides as he worked himself over and over into Piper. The grip of her inner walls were as tight as vice grips.

"Give it to me, Brandon."

"Shit."

Piper, a known cougar, performed like a horny twenty-two year old. Her pussy was flaming hot. Its inner juices were overflowing. Her clit was throbbing. Underneath her back and with her legs spread, the sheets were soaked from her multiple orgasms. She'd bussed all over Brandon's dick more times than she could remember.

Brandon now had one of Piper's legs locked with his arm as he tightly cradled the back of her in the crook of his elbow. In that position, she couldn't maneuver or escape. She could only take his pounding. Knowing she couldn't escape, he dug harder and more forcefully.

"Ahhhhhhhhhhh, Brandon!" she screamed.

Growling like a lion, he grinded himself in the pussy with very long strokes, and a wide smirk. As he did, his body was drenched in sweat. Brandon prided himself on being an exceptional lover. He called it a gift from God, especially his ability to go all night. He'd been stroking for at least two hours trying to punish Piper. The pussy was so good though he couldn't help fighting his yearning for an orgasm.

"Brandon, oh, oh, oh, ohhhhhhhhh, I'm cumming!"

Brandon dug harder. He could feel his orgasm building as Piper released. Since he had been holding back longer than usual he knew it was going to be a big one. He knew it was going to be huge.

"Give it to me, Brandon. Give me that nut!"

Thrusting ferociously, Brandon began to beat the pussy up with a vengeance. He could feel certain muscles in his back and thighs beginning to cramp. He wouldn't let up though. He was too close. He needed to let off.

"Oh, shit, Brandon. Fuck me, young buck. Give me all that cum, baby!"

Finally...

Brandon exploded. He let loose with a gushing orgasm that easily put previous ones to shame. He released so much cum that his thirty year old body immediately felt exhausted. He had no choice but to collapse beside Piper.

Needing to recuperate, Piper reached for her sanity package, her weed; several blunts had been rolled already. A moment after lighting up, she stared up at the ceiling satisfied. She was always satisfied after a session with Brandon. He always knew how to fuck her, the right way. He always knew exactly which spots to hit.

Unbeknownst to everyone, Brandon and Piper had begun fucking shortly after Mr. Bishop left her for Chetti. It began five years ago as a nurturing friendship, with Brandon consoling Piper's broken heart; in time though it turned sexual. The two fell out of touch shortly after but began speaking again several months ago mainly due to Piper needing an eye kept on Nessa. She discovered then that Brandon had ulterior motives for his family also.

He wanted a bigger piece of the pie.

He wanted to be king.

In fact, he really did know about the Federal investigation. He also knew about the raid. He just chose to keep it secret. Getting Luke, Chetti and Darien off the street would work in his favor. And the fact that Luke now wanted Nessa to be involved in his business made things even better.

"So, are you sure they're going to let Nessa out tonight?" Piper asked, exhaling smoke to the ceiling of the motel room.

"Definitely."

Piper looked closely at Brandon. Narrowing her eyes she asked, "Are you fucking my daughter?"

"What?"

"You heard me."

"Piper, you're tripping."

Rising up and giving Brandon a no nonsense glare, Piper asked again, "Brandon, are you fucking my daughter?"

"No, Piper. Why the fuck would you say something like that?"

"Are you sure?"

"Piper, I said, no. Besides, Luke would kill me if I did something like that."

"Well, you'd better not be. I know the lil' bitch is

216

sexy but your job is to simply keep an eye on her, stir the pot and make sure she's doing what she's supposed to."

"I got you, Piper. Don't worry about it."

"She still doesn't know that you and I know each other, right?"

"Right," Brandon stated with frustration.

"I'm serious, Brandon. You haven't told her nothing?"

"Of course I haven't."

"I'm dead serious. I have to know I can trust her. I have to know she won't lie to me about a single penny. If she knows you're watching her on my behalf, she'll cover her ass if she has plans on crossing me."

"She's your daughter, Piper. She won't cross you."

"All that sounds good but I still have to be sure."

"Out of curiosity, if she does cross you, then what?"

Flashes of what Piper had done to Charles appeared in her head. Seeing the flame of the blowtorch and hearing the blast of the gunshots, she said, "For her sake, let's just hope it doesn't come to that. I refuse to be betrayed again."

"Well, she doesn't know about me and you. And she's handling her business. I was worried about her falling for Luke a little too much though. But after showing her the photos of him cheating, it's obvious she hates his guts.

"And what about the accessory charges they have on her?"

"She's good. They don't have evidence of her being involved in anything. She'll walk." Brandon checked the cheap watch on his wrist. "As a matter of fact she gets out in a couple hours. We should both be at County by then. I've got to check on the others."

"Okay."

"And don't worry. The million we're going to get from the stash is only the beginning. We're all about to become multimillionaires."

The two pulled each other close.

"It's all going to work out, Piper," Brandon said. "You'll get your revenge. Their empire is ours for the taking."

Those words eased Piper's worries.

After nastily fondling each other and going for another round of sex, the two showered together. An hour later, they parted ways. Piper herself headed to the County Jail to pick up Nessa. Arriving, she pulled to the curb and stepped slowly out of the car. She was clearly faded after smoking one more time before leaving the motel, but noticed several other people waiting for love ones, too. Some people waited near the prisoner release staircase while others were a few yards away where people entered the facility.

Thirty minutes later, Piper found herself standing on the sidewalk glancing at her watch, and smoking yet another cigarette. She'd become irritated and wanted to know what in the hell was taking so long. Suddenly, a door opened at the top of the County Jail's staircase. Nessa appeared and began to make her way down the steps. Piper smiled at the thought of producing such a gorgeous human being, but was filled with slight envy at the same time. There was something about Nessa's style and confidence that she wanted to mimic.

"Damn, girl, what took so long?" Piper asked as Nessa reached the bottom of the steps.

The two women, basically spitting images of each other; one older, one younger, were now face to face.

"That's a stupid question. I was waiting for them to release me."

Taking a final pull of her cigarette, dropping the butt to the sidewalk and stepping on it, Piper asked her daughter, "Uhmmm… Well, where are we?"

Smiling, Nessa answered, "A slight change in plans but we're still good."

"How good?"

"A million dollars richer. But that's just to start with. And if everything goes well, Chetti will spend the rest of her life in prison."

Piper smiled. Those words were music to her ears. Her daughter hadn't fucked up too bad. "Bingo!" Piper blasted.

They both turned to see Sidra walking up on them. Quickly, she wrapped her arms around Nessa.

"Bitch, I was sooooo worried about yo ass," Sidra began. "So, who we fuckin' up first?" she asked, glancing at Piper and giving her the once over.

Nessa smiled, loving the support her girl always gave her. She was always there, no matter what. "Thanks for coming to see about me," she told her. "I got lots of shit to bring you up to speed on."

Piper hated hearing Nessa seem so close to anyone but her. She knew that the two girls had been friends since childhood; still she trusted no one. Seconds later, a Crown Victoria pulled to the curb a distance ahead of Piper's car. A moment later, Brandon stepped out and began to make his way up the County Jail's steps to its entrance. Seeing him, Nessa called out, "Brandon!"

He turned to her.

Nessa ran toward him, telling her mother to wait by the car. Reaching him, she threw her arms around him and said, "Thank you."

Looking over Nessa's shoulder at Piper and seeing a glare, he quickly pulled away from Nessa and said, "Don't worry about it. I told you I'd take care of everything."

"Have you found out anything about Cedrick and

Trinity?" she asked.

He shook his head. "I'm definitely looking into it though."

"Brandon, I'm not lying. I know what I saw. Cedrick is alive."

"I believe you"

Brandon really did believe her and he really was going to look into the situation. If he could find Cedrick quickly, that could be more ammunition to keep The Bishops locked up.

"But that aside," he continued. "Are you prepared for what you're about to get into?"

"Of course."

"Nessa, come the fuck on!" Piper shouted.

Nessa flipped her hand sharply letting her mother know she wasn't ready yet. The entire moment of being close to Nessa while Piper watched made Brandon uncomfortable.

Looking her directly in the eyes, he said, "I'm not sure you understand what's happening here. This isn't a game. The Bishops didn't make it to the top overnight and without getting blood on their hands. There was a lot of betrayal, a lot of murder."

"I can handle it."

"Shit's getting crazy, Nessa. Over the past several days, Chetti has been having her men killed; drivers, bodyguards, runners, men who have been with the family for decades. She's been having them all killed from her cell just to keep them quiet. One was just discovered hanging in his jail cell a moment ago. I'm on my way up there now. That's how powerful and vicious she is. And if she discovers *any betrayal on your end*, Nessa, *you'll* be next."

Nessa didn't show it but those words sent chills down her spine.

"When she finds out that Luke is snitching on her, and you're out here making moves on Luke's behalf, or at least pretending to be, she's going to put a hit on you. That means every killer in the city is going to come after you. That's going to complicate your rise to the top. Shit's about to get crazy, Nessa. Trust me."

Nessa hadn't quite thought about all of that before. She now knew she'd have to count on NaNa and Juicy for help.

"With great power comes great responsibility, Nessa. You sure you're ready for that responsibility?"

Silence.

Passing moments.

Several faces appeared in Nessa's mind: her father, Chetti, Luke and Darien. Each were ultimately about to become enemies, enemies she knew would need to be dealt with if she was going to become the queen of the streets. She realized exactly what she had to do.

"Well?" Brandon asked.

"I'm ready to do what I need to do. And when the time comes, I'll take Chetti out if I have to," she finally answered.

"What?"

"You heard me. I'm going to take that bitch out. You just said that she's going to come after me, right? Well, I'm not going to depend on the justice system to keep her locked up. That won't do me any good if she still has power from her cell. I don't have a choice except to take her ass out before she does me."

Brandon didn't say anything.

"And if Luke and Darien get in my way, they'll go too. I want these streets, Brandon. And I'm willing to do whatever it'll take to get them."

Brandon breathed a heavy sigh. "And one other

thing..."

"What?"

He lowered his head, unable to look Nessa in the face.

"What? What is it?" she asked again.

"Chetti knows we were at the Ritz together. I'm sure it won't be long before she tells Luke."

Nessa's heart sank. She took several breaths and said, "We'll cross that road when the time comes. For now, set up the meetings, and let's get started."

Seeing Piper watching him again, Brandon ended the conversation and rushed to the top of the stairs, entering the facility. He didn't want any issues with Piper. As Nessa turned to leave she felt good about her plan to become filthy rich. All seemed to be going as planned until she noticed her father slowly, and sneakily climbing the stairs to enter the jail. The moment they made eye contact, Nessa understood clearly his intent.

Oh, shit, he's going to let them know what happened with Luke's father.

Nessa dashed up the steps to catch up with her father. Catching him in the lobby, she asked, "What the hell are you doing here?"

"What the fuck do you think?" he asked. "You played me. You were supposed to come through on our agreement and you didn't. Well, since you want to play games, let's see how funny it is when I make sure this video makes it into Luke's hands and the cops." He headed off.

Nessa grabbed his arm. "I was in jail. What the fuck?"

"No excuse," he spewed back while snatching away from her. "Before you were arrested, you had plenty of time. Well, I'm done with your bullshit. The cops are getting this video and definitely Luke." There was fury in his bloodshot eyes.

Grabbing his arm again and pulling him towards the door, she lowered her tone so no one else could hear what she was about to say except she and her father. She then said, "Look, I'm working on something big, really fucking big.

"Like what?"

"Don't worry about it. Just know that I'm going to handle what I've got to handle with you."

With no tolerance for lies and games, he pressed closely against her, stared seriously into her eyes and said, "Listen here, you little sneaky bitch. Whatever you're working on, I'm giving you only 72 hours to get me two hundred fifty thousand dollars."

Looking at him like he'd lost his fucking mind, she said in almost a yell, "Two hundred fifty thousand dollars? Are you crazy? What kinda father are you?"

"You never wanted a father before, why now? Nevermind…don't answer that. I just want my fuckin' money. I know that rich boyfriend of yours has money stashed away somewhere. All drug dealers like him do. So that combined with whatever thing you're working on should make it easy to get my damn money?"

Nessa was furious. She'd always had a deep hatred for him but even more now. She wanted to murder his ass.

Smirking and enjoying that he'd gotten underneath her skin, he told her, "72 hours, baby girl. If I don't have my money by then, this video goes to the cops and your boy."

With that said, he walked away.

Wanting to snap, Nessa stood there in the lobby alone. Shit had gotten so complicated so quickly: Chetti possibly wanting her dead, her father threatening to give the murder video to the cops. Shit had gotten crazy with major problems already, and she hadn't even been out of jail for ten damn minutes. Stressed and shaking her head over it, after several moments she finally sucked it all up and headed out of the building. Making her way down the steps with her head held high, she said to herself, "Since Chetti and my deadbeat ass daddy want war with me, that's exactly what I'm going to give them."

CHECK OUT THESE TITLES
BY: *Kendall Banks*

In Stores Now

MAIL TO:
PO Box 423
Brandywine, MD 20613
301-362-6508

ORDER FORM

| Ship to: |
| Address: |

| Date: | Phone: |
| Email: |

| City & State: | Zip: |

Make all money orders and cashiers checks payable to: **Life Changing Books**

Qty.	ISBN	Title	Release Date	Price
	0-9741394-2-4	Bruised by Azarel	Jul-05	$ 15.00
	0-9741394-7-5	Bruised 2: The Ultimate Revenge by Azarel	Oct-06	$ 15.00
	0-9741394-3-2	Secrets of a Housewife by J. Tremble	Feb-06	$ 15.00
	0-9741394-6-7	The Millionaire Mistress by Tiphani	Nov-06	$ 15.00
	1-934230-99-5	More Secrets More Lies by J. Tremble	Feb-07	$ 15.00
	1-934230-95-2	A Private Affair by Mike Warren	May-07	$ 15.00
	1-934230-96-0	Flexin & Sexin Volume 1	Jun-07	$ 15.00
	1-934230-89-8	Still a Mistress by Tiphani	Nov-07	$ 15.00
	1-934230-91-X	Daddy's House by Azarel	Nov-07	$ 15.00
	1-934230-88-X	Naughty Little Angel by J. Tremble	Feb-08	$ 15.00
	1-934230820	Rich Girls by Kendall Banks	Oct-08	$ 15.00
	1-934230839	Expensive Taste by Tiphani	Nov-08	$ 15.00
	1-934230782	Brooklyn Brothel by C. Stecko	Jan-09	$ 15.00
	1-934230669	Good Girl Gone bad by Danette Majette	Mar-09	$ 15.00
	1-934230804	From Hood to Hollywood by Sasha Raye	Mar-09	$ 15.00
	1-934230707	Sweet Swagger by Mike Warren	Jun-09	$ 15.00
	1-934230677	Carbon Copy by Azarel	Jul-09	$ 15.00
	1-934230723	Millionaire Mistress 3 by Tiphani	Nov-09	$ 15.00
	1-934230715	A Woman Scorned by Ericka Williams	Nov-09	$ 15.00
	1-934230685	My Man Her Son by J. Tremble	Feb-10	$ 15.00
	1-924230731	Love Heist by Jackie D.	Mar-10	$ 15.00
	1-934230812	Flexin & Sexin Volume 2	Apr-10	$ 15.00
	1-934230748	The Dirty Divorce by Miss KP	May-10	$ 15.00
	1-934230758	Chedda Boyz by CJ Hudson	Jul-10	$ 15.00
	1-934230766	Snitch by VegasClarke	Oct-10	$ 15.00
	1-934230693	Money Maker by Tonya Ridley	Oct-10	$ 15.00
	1-934230774	The Dirty Divorce Part 2 by Miss KP	Nov-10	$ 15.00
	1-934230170	The Available Wife by Carla Pennington	Jan-11	$ 15.00
	1-934230774	One Night Stand by Kendall Banks	Feb-11	$ 15.00
	1-934230278	Bitter by Danette Majette	Feb-11	$ 15.00
	1-934230299	Married to a Balla by Jackie D.	May-11	$ 15.00
	1-934230308	The Dirty Divorce Part 3 by Miss KP	Jun-11	$ 15.00
	1-934230316	Next Door Nympho By CJ Hudson	Jun-11	$ 15.00
	1-934230286	Bedroom Gangsta by J. Tremble	Sep-11	$ 15.00
	1-934230340	Another One Night Stand by Kendall Banks	Oct-11	$ 15.00
	1-934230359	The Available Wife. Part 2 by Carla Pennington	Nov-11	$ 15.00
	1-934230332	Wealthy & Wicked by Chris Renee	Jan-12	$ 15.00
	1-934230375	Life After a Balla by Jackie D.	Mar-12	$ 15.00
	1-934230251	V.I.P. by Azarel	Apr-12	$ 15.00
	1-934230383	Welfare Grind by Kendall Banks	May-12	$ 15.00
	1-934230413	Still Grindin' by Kendall Banks	Sep-12	$ 15.00
	1-934230391	Paparazzi by Miss KP	Oct-13	$ 15.00
	1-93423043X	Cashin' Out by Jai Nicole	Nov-12	$ 15.00
	1-934230634	Welfare Grind Part 3 by Kendall Banks	Mar-13	$15.00
	1-934230642	Game Over by Winter Ramos	Apr-13	$15.99
	1-934230618	My Counterfeit Husband by Carla Pennington	Aug-14	$ 15.00
	1-93423060X	Mistress Loose	Oct-13	$ 15.00
	1-934230626	Dirty Divorce Part 4	Jan-14	$ 15.00
			Total for Books	$
		Shipping Charges (add $4.95 for 1-4 books*)		$
			Total Enclosed (add lines)	$

* Prison Orders- Please allow up to three (3) weeks for delivery.

Please Note: We are not held responsible for returned prison orders. Make sure the facility will receive books before ordering.

*Shipping and Handling of 5-10 books is $6.95, please contact us if your order is more than 10 books.
(301)362-6508